Some things ar[e]
hide...even in t[he...]

A feathery sensation running up and down Cat's arm coaxed her to wakefulness. She could barely see the man sitting next to her on the bed, but her other senses compensated.

The mattress dipped as his weight shifted. She felt his inquisitive touch on her face, a whisper of sensation. His fingers moved to her throat, and lower, skimming over her breasts. "This is some nightgown," he murmured.

She cleared her throat. "I was hoping you'd like it." Even though she'd expected him, now that he was actually there, she was nervous.

Mustering her courage, Cat offered a quavery smile, though she knew he couldn't see it. "Don't feel that you have to spend a lot of time on conversation or, um—" she swallowed hard "—foreplay."

For the longest time he said nothing, and then, "I don't think this is such a good idea. Don't take it personally, but I'm just not into it."

"Yes, well, I'm so sorry to disappoint you." Mortified, she tried to spring off the bed, but he caught both her arms.

"Just for the record," he said, then his mouth seized hers, his arm banded around her back, crushing her to him, and he kissed her with an intensity that left no doubt that he wanted her...badly. you knew Greg wasn't coming?"

Dear Reader,

What pops into your mind when you read the words *wrong bed?* No, I'm not referring to your mother-in-law's convertible sofa bed with the lumpy mattress and the bar that digs into your spine. Use your imagination. Put together a him and a her and a bed. Now throw a monkey wrench into the works.

That's what I did when Temptation asked me to write a "Wrong Bed" story. This is one of the most fun and sexy miniseries ever. It's an anything-goes concept that has inspired wonderful stories from some of Harlequin's favorite authors.

Once I started thinking about guys and gals and wrong beds, it didn't take me long to come up with *In the Dark,* about a woman who desperately wants to become pregnant—without the unwelcome burden of a husband—and comes up with a foolproof scheme to do just that. Funny thing about foolproof schemes, though. They have a way of blowing up in your face.

I'd love to know what you thought of Cat and Brody—and even Spot the geriatric mutt! Write to me at P.O. Box 1321, North Baldwin, NY 11510-0721 (please include an SASE for reply). If you have access to the Internet, visit my home page by going to Harlequin's web site (http://www.romance.net) and clicking on my name on the author list.

Enjoy!

Pamela Burford

P.S. In April look for the next "Wrong Bed" story, #727 *Tangled Sheets* by Jo Leigh.

IN THE DARK
Pamela Burford

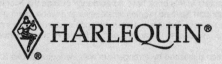

HARLEQUIN®

TORONTO • NEW YORK • LONDON
AMSTERDAM • PARIS • SYDNEY • HAMBURG
STOCKHOLM • ATHENS • TOKYO • MILAN • MADRID
PRAGUE • WARSAW • BUDAPEST • AUCKLAND

To my wonderful editor,
Susan Sheppard.

ISBN 0-373-25823-2

IN THE DARK

Printed in U.S.A.

OKAY, so maybe I'm a little nervous, Cat Seabright admitted to herself as she wiped her damp palms on her cotton sundress. Why deny it? What was going to happen in this apartment to-night would, after all, transform her life forever. She hoped.

She leaned on the warm metal railing of the penthouse terrace and stared at the sparkling cityscape of Manhattan's Upper East Side at night. The spacious top-floor terrace offered a panoramic view of lofty buildings stretching into the distance, all studded with innumerable glowing windows.

Muted sounds of traffic from the street twenty-two floors below competed with the se-ductive drone of the apartment's air conditioner behind her. There wasn't a whiff of breeze to stir the heavy, muggy air. The July heat was nearly as oppressive now, after ten at night, as it had been at high noon.

Cat resisted checking her watch, knowing it had been only about a minute and a half since she'd last done so. He wouldn't arrive for per-haps another half hour yet—*if* his plane had landed on time and *if* he'd managed to get a taxi promptly and *if* that taxi wasn't now sitting in snarled traffic on the bridge or in the tunnel. If, if, if.

Just get here, Greg. Get here and let's just do it before I lose my nerve.

No. She wouldn't lose her nerve. It would be awkward, certainly, and mechanical, but the end result was what mattered.

As Cat gazed distractedly at the glittering urban landscape, a block of buildings to the north abruptly disappeared—or seemed to as the windows winked into darkness. She straightened and stared, wide-eyed, as the lights in an adjacent cluster of buildings disappeared. Within seconds everything north blinked out, as far as she could see, then the West Side in one great swath, and then her own chunk of the city suddenly turned dark.

The air conditioner rumbled to silence as Cat stood frozen. "A blackout," she whispered. A real, honest-to-goodness New York City blackout! The day's record heat must have placed the ultimate strain on the city's power system.

From street level far below came a cacophony of human voices, a faint mumble that swiftly rose in volume. New Yorkers roaring their delight or disgust, or possibly both.

A blackout. No electricity to run the elevator. Which meant Greg would have to climb twenty-two flights of stairs to get to her. That thought had her sputtering with nervous laughter as she turned and made her way across the brick-paved terrace, which felt like a pizza oven under the bare soles of her feet.

Yep, that's me, she thought, *the most alluring*

babe in New York. A woman any man would traverse the continent for, before cheerfully sprinting up twenty-two flights of stairs. With luggage. There she was, the fairy-tale princess in her forbidding tower, devising a fitting test of endurance for all those princes clamoring for her hand in marriage.

No, not marriage, she reminded herself, as she stepped through the doorway into the cool, dark living room and groped her way around the velvet-upholstered sofa. It had taken long enough—thirty-eight years, to be precise—but Cat had eventually given up that particular pipe dream. There was only one thing she really wanted out of life, and she'd finally decided she'd waited for it long enough.

Has anyone thought to lay in a few candles here? she wondered, gingerly making her way through the gloom to the small kitchen, barking her shin on the marble coffee table in the process.

What would Nana do if she knew Cat had appropriated the agency's apartment for the night? And for such a scandalous purpose? She wouldn't be amused, that was for sure. Cat's employer was as straitlaced as they came, hence the grandmotherly moniker. One of her first clients had nicknamed Mrs. Amaryllis Littlestone "Nana" and the name had stuck.

Nana would fire Cat if she knew about tonight; end of story. Nana's "nurturers" were expected to comport themselves in a chaste and dignified manner, in their off hours as well as on assignment.

Up until now, Cat had never had a problem living up to her employer's exacting standards. She was anything but a hell-raiser, and her pitifully tame love life wouldn't raise an eyebrow. In the kitchen, she felt for a drawer handle and began to carefully paw through corkscrews and chopsticks, blindly hunting for a candle and praying she wouldn't find a boning knife or an ice pick in the process.

Cat had actually admitted to Greg on the phone that she hadn't had sex in three years. She still couldn't decide whether that particular item of information was likely to turn him on or, heaven forbid, earn his pity.

"Oh yeah, that's what you want to be," she muttered as she slammed the drawer shut and fumbled for the one next to it, "the kind of woman men sleep with out of pity."

She'd located the junk drawer, and it bore fruit: a short candle stub, the remnant, no doubt, of some intimate *dîner tête à tête*. A little more exploring turned up a mostly empty matchbook and a squat, wax-encrusted glass candlestick. She crammed the candle in the holder and touched a lit match to the blackened wick.

"We're in business—romantic lighting," she dryly intoned. "Ha ha ha."

Whatever this night held in store for her, she was pretty certain "romantic" wasn't part of the equation. Though the experience should shape up as a great story to tell her child someday.

You were conceived on the night of the big New York City blackout. Your daddy had to trudge up twenty-two flights of stairs because he'd promised to try and make a baby with Mommy while Mommy could still make babies.

All right, so maybe she'd stick to the three little pigs. As bedtime stories went, this particular escapade left something to be desired.

Like a husband.

No. She wouldn't travel that mental road again, and the dead end it inevitably led to. Her two-decade search for Mr. Perfect had been a resounding failure. He didn't exist. Neither did Mr. Almost-perfect or even Mr. What-the-heck-it's-worth-a-try.

Brigit claimed Cat's requirements in a mate were too exacting, that she was holding out for some impossible-to-attain ideal. Cat's answer was always the same. Considering the alarming divorce rate nowadays, was it possible to be too picky? The last thing Cat would want to do was subject some innocent child to the emotional meat grinder of divorce, having experienced that particular hell firsthand.

Cat carried the lit candle into the bedroom and set it on the dresser next to the huge gourmet snack basket wrapped in cellophane. The contents looked tempting—everything from Godiva chocolates to blue corn chips—but she didn't dare touch it. She had to leave this place precisely the way she'd found it or risk Nana discovering she'd been here.

When she left tomorrow, the agency's apartment would have been restored to its previous condition, but as for herself...

Cat's hand drifted to her abdomen. If tonight was a success and she did indeed become pregnant, her job would be forfeit within a few months anyway, once she showed. A pregnant unmarried lady? Not in Nana's agency. But in the meantime Cat would continue to work and save every nickel toward a house in the suburbs. She had no intention of raising her child in her apartment in Tarrytown, the upper floor of a two-family house. She'd never even considered trying to conceive the baby there, under the watchful eyes and keen ears of her landlady, Mrs. Santangelo.

Selecting a suitable location had been the easy part, and she was certain Nana wouldn't notice that the spare set of apartment keys was missing from her office before Cat could return them. Selecting a suitable sperm donor, on the other hand…

Thank goodness for Brigit. Her best friend had come through for her. They'd been sitting in the Magnolia Coffee Shop last month, their favorite breakfast spot, discussing Cat's plight over Belgian waffles and the Magnolia's bottomless cup of coffee. By that point Brigit had given up trying to persuade her lifelong friend of the foolhardiness of her scheme and they were in the process of vetting candidates for the honor of Chief Inseminator. The guy had to have exemplary genes, but just as important, he had to be willing to stay out of the picture once the deed was done.

One by one they'd crossed off the names Brigit had scrawled on her paper place mat, until only two remained: Cat's old boyfriend Anton

Lind, a confirmed bachelor, and Brigit's cousin Greg Bannister.

Cat had been tempted to choose Anton, who had the distinction of being the hottest guy she'd ever dated, with his golden Viking beauty and body by Nautilus. Mentally melding her own coppery curls and his pale locks, she envisioned a darling little girl with strawberry blond hair and the pale blue eyes both parents shared. And Anton was convenient; he lived right there in the city. More important, she'd slept with him before. Of course, it had been a long time ago, about four years, but at least he was a known quantity. They had a history.

Which was why she'd ultimately crossed Anton off the list. The last thing she needed was her baby's biological father running into them at the park, wistfully recalling the relationship they'd once shared, dropping by for unexpected visits. Confirmed bachelor or not, she could see him becoming nostalgic for the good old days and renewing their emotional involvement once they'd made a baby together.

That left Greg, Brigit's Cute Cousin, which was how Cat had thought of him the one and only time she'd met him, at her and Brigit's high school graduation. He'd been twenty-two then, tall and handsome, with a confident, easygoing manner so at odds with the blustering immaturity of the boys her own age.

Nevertheless, she hadn't thought of Greg in twenty years, until Brigit had offered him up for stud service.

"He'd do it," Brigit had stated with confidence. "Greg is the most laid-back guy I know. And I mean, he's even hotter now than he was back when you met him. If he weren't my cousin, *I'd* jump him!"

A one-night stand with the Cute Cousin. Oh my. "He lives in Alaska, right?" Cat had asked.

"Yep—settled there after college. He's an engineer, something to do with the oil pipeline. You know," Brigit had added with a suggestive smirk, "I hear there are a lot more men than women in Alaska. You just know that boy's gonna be *ready* for you. He'll get the job done in one shot."

After that, the arrangements had been fairly straightforward. Brigit had run the idea past Greg, who did indeed remember Cat—"the red-head with the granny glasses, right?"

I wear contacts now, she'd wanted to tell him, as if that made a difference. The important thing was, he'd agreed to do it. When Brigit had put Cat on the phone, Greg had told her he was scheduled to fly into New York soon, on a date that coincided with Cat's fertile time of the month, as it turned out. Talk about kismet!

If she didn't get pregnant tonight, Cat thought, stripping off her sundress and underwear, she was back to square one. Because unless she was willing to fly to Alaska for another try with Greg—an expensive proposition—she'd have to find someone else.

Before getting into the shower, she slipped on her seersucker robe and placed the keys under the welcome mat in front of the apartment door. She was glad now that she'd thought to tell Greg to look for them there, in case she didn't answer the doorbell. If his plane was delayed, she might be asleep when he arrived.

She took a short, cool shower, washing the sweat and grime of the sweltering day off her body. She didn't linger under the spray, knowing that the building's water pump was out of commission for the duration of the blackout; the only water available to the upper floors was whatever remained in the rooftop tank.

Cat finished toweling off in the bedroom, staring at the negligee she'd laid out on the bed, wishing she'd packed something less...actually, something *more*. More fabric, more coverage. More modesty. She sighed deeply. This scrap of deep green silk had been a gift from Brigit, a good-luck token for what Cat's friend undoubtedly envisioned as a night of unbridled passion. All Brigit had requested in exchange was a full accounting. "I mean all the juicy details, girl. I want to be able to picture every drop of sweat."

Imagine, someone getting vicarious thrills hearing about Caitlin Seabright's love life. "Ha ha ha," she said, as she lifted the filmy garment and slipped it over her head. It slithered over her body and fell to her ankles with a muted whisper of gossamer silk.

Cat examined her image in the mirrored closet door by candlelight. Flimsy little spaghetti straps were all that held the thing up. A side slit exposed one leg practically to the hipbone. The neckline of the sheer mesh bodice plunged nearly to her navel, secured with a silk cord that crisscrossed through little loops that only went as high as the undersides of her breasts.

She yanked the cord as tight as possible, but the sides of the bodice refused to meet. No doubt that was the intention. She tied a bow under her bust and glanced at her reflection—and blinked in awe.

The corsetlike lacing caused the gown to hug her torso. And it did something truly remarkable to her breasts, which she'd always thought of as, well, as pretty unremarkable. It crowded them together and hiked them up until they practically burst out of the skimpy bits of fabric that theoretically were supposed to cover them. Even by candlelight her nipples were clearly visible beneath the sheer dark green mesh.

"I can't wear this," Cat whispered. She turned; the side view was equally majestic. "Can I?" She'd never owned a nightgown like this, a garment that had absolutely nothing to do with sleeping. Good grief, what would Greg think of her?

What did he already think of her, a single woman who'd arranged to be impregnated by a virtual stranger? She struck a pose, one hand on her hip. The long slit parted to reveal the entire length of her leg. Tugging off her hair scrunchie to release her ponytail, she shook her head and watched her wavy red hair fluff around her face, just grazing her bare shoulders.

Cat had never seen herself like this, as some sort of seductress. She couldn't deny the heady sensation that had her adjusting the gown's bodice to see just how outrageously provocative she could make herself look.

What would it hurt to play the part, just for one night? she thought, lifting her hair at the nape and watching other parts of herself lift as well. With luck, she wouldn't even see Greg again after tonight. Did it really matter what he thought of her?

Yes. Anything was better than pity.

"Well, that's settled, then," she told her X-rated reflection. "For one night you get to be Delilah." Then it was on to the glory and glamour of diaper rash and strained peas.

Cat had kept the windows closed as long as possible, trying to hold in the residual coolness, but it was getting warmer by the minute with the air conditioner off. She went around opening them now, letting in the humid outside air and the faraway street noise. She thought she heard the crash of breaking glass, and wondered how much looting damage the morning would reveal. She loved the city, but sometimes she hated it, too.

She flopped onto the queen-size bed, over the quilted bedspread, and grabbed a magazine off the nightstand to fan herself with. Looking down at her supine form, she marveled that everything was as high and perky as when she'd been standing. A miracle of engineering, this nightie. Greg would probably want to study it carefully, she mused, smiling around a yawn. He was, after all, some sort of engineer. Another plus—good gray-matter genes to pass on to Junior.

The candle stub still burned, but there wasn't enough light to read by. All she had to occupy her mind was her own nervous anticipation. She would have been a fraction cooler without the skimpy negligee, but she drew the line at waiting for Greg in the altogether.

She squirmed, trying to find a comfortable position in the heat. Fighting back another yawn, she let her eyes drift shut, just for a moment.

A FEATHERY SENSATION running up and down Cat's arm coaxed her to wakefulness. After a while it stopped and she felt fingers on her brow, stroking her hair.

She opened her eyes and came fully awake with a start. A big hand settled on her shoulder, heavy and reassuring. The room was pitch-dark, except for the faintest glimmer of moonlight from the wide-open windows. The candle must have burned out while she'd slept.

She could barely see the man sitting next to her on the bed, but her other senses compensated. She detected the warmth radiating from his large body. The subtle, agreeable scent of fresh sweat on clean skin brought to mind all those stairs. A hint of tobacco smoke clung to his clothes.

"I figured you'd want me to wake you." His voice was a low, rich murmur. "You must've dozed off waiting for me."

She nodded, and realizing he couldn't see her any better than she could see him, said, "Yeah, I...I guess I did."

Even though she'd expected him, now that he

was actually there, the enormity of what she was about to do became a great weight, paralyzing her.

"Traffic is an unholy mess, with no street-lights and the party animals out in force," Greg said. "I couldn't stand inching along, so I ditched the taxi and walked the last few blocks."

He probably wasn't even aware he was rub-bing her upper arm as he spoke. It was the inti-mate caress of a friend, not a stranger. Well, this wasn't the first time they'd met, after all. Cat felt herself relax fractionally—a small miracle con-sidering the nature of this rendezvous and the fact that she was wearing the most brazenly sex-ual getup Brigit Bannister had been able to find. And Brigit knew where to look.

For the first time, Cat was thankful for the blackout.

"I'm sorry you had to walk up all those stairs," she said.

Cat sensed he was smiling. She had the dis-tinct impression this man spent a lot of time do-ing that.

"Not your fault," he said. "Unless you're somehow responsible for the blackout?"

She felt herself returning his smile. "Well, I *was* running the air conditioner."

"That had to be what did it." He chuckled, the sound somehow bold and impish at once. Cat knew that if there was a shortage of women in Alaska, it was because they were all flocking to this man.

Tentatively she reached out to touch his face,

and encountered his jaw, rough with beard
stubble.

"You're trembling!" he said, closing his warm
fingers over her icy hands.

Well, what did he expect—nerves of steel? He
pressed a tender kiss to the backs of her fingers,
then to the tips. She was unprepared for the feel
of his mouth, like sun-warmed satin.

The scanty moonlight hinted at bold masculine features and short, dark hair that was a bit
unruly on top, as if the waves refused to be
tamed. Twenty years ago Greg had worn his
hair fairly long, enhancing his boyish good
looks. This shorter cut no doubt complemented
the rugged maturity the past two decades had
carved into his face.

Sensing his eyes on her, she speculated that
perhaps Greg possessed better night vision than
she. The mattress dipped as his weight shifted.
She felt his inquisitive touch on her face, a whisper of sensation tickling her eyelashes. He
traced her nose, her mouth, the shape of her
chin. His fingers moved to her throat, and lower,
skimming over her breasts without the slightest
hesitation. Cat held her breath, knowing Greg
felt the frantic drumming of her heart and wishing she could be as blasé as he. Far from sharing
her agitation, he seemed sublimely at ease.

"This is some outfit," he said, toying with the
crisscrossed lacing.

She cleared her throat. "I was hoping you'd
like it."

"I like it. Wish I could see it." His hand glided
down her rib cage to her hip and thigh, treating

the rest of her to the same unhurried inspection. The feverish imprint of his fingers seemed to linger everywhere he touched.

Mustering her courage, Cat sat up and moved over, making room for him to stretch out on the bed. She offered a quavery smile, though she knew he couldn't see it. "Don't feel that you have to spend a lot of time on conversation or, um—" she swallowed hard "—foreplay. We can just, you know, get down to it. If you want."

For the longest time Greg said nothing. She searched his shadowed features, in vain. Finally he said, "I don't think this is such a good idea."

His words struck her like a fist to the gut. "What? You...you don't want to...?"

"I'm just not into it. Don't take it personally."

Humiliation scalded her face and stung her eyes. He'd changed his mind. He'd come all this way, climbed all those stairs, for one purpose only—and now, now that he'd gotten to *inspect* the woman he was supposed to make a baby with...

"But it's...it's all arranged." Her voice climbed a couple of octaves. "I mean, if we're not going to have sex, then what am I doing here?" She tugged at the bodice of her negligee in an inane effort to cover herself.

"We both know this wasn't my idea." His tone was not unkind, which somehow made it all the harder to bear.

"Yes, well, I'm so sorry to disappoint you. Excuse me." She started to rise, but he stopped her.

"Hold on. Is that what you think? That I don't find you desirable?"

"Don't worry," she snapped. "I won't take it *personally*. She tried to spring off the bed, but he caught both her arms. She turned her head, unable to face him even in the dark.

"Just so we understand one another," he said, "it's not you. It's the circumstances." She didn't respond, and it soon became clear he wouldn't release her until she did.

At last she said, "The circumstances?"

"I'm accustomed to being the…initiator, I guess you'd say. This sort of thing just goes against my grain. Trust me." Slowly he trailed one knuckle down her throat and along her freshly minted cleavage. "I find you very desirable."

The simple caress stole Cat's breath. She felt her nipples tighten against the silk mesh covering them. Her body's response shamed her. If Greg truly thought she was so damn desirable, he'd do what he'd come here to do, what he'd promised to do, bizarre "circumstances" notwithstanding. Brigit had described her cousin as the most laid-back guy she knew. He'd said nothing on the phone to indicate he had a problem with the circumstances.

She supposed she should be grateful. At least he wasn't sleeping with her out of pity!

Cat pushed his hands away. "Look, thanks for the gallant effort, but you don't have to lie to spare my feelings. I know I'm nothing special."

"Gallant, huh? Never been accused of that one before." Without warning he grabbed her hand and brought it to his crotch. Reflexively she tried to pull away, but he held her palm firmly against the distended fly of his jeans.

His erection felt enormous under her hand, as rigid as a wooden club. His fingers wrapped around hers, forcing her to measure the length and breadth of his arousal. For a moment she was too stunned to move, to breathe. Even her heartbeat seemed to falter.

Greg leaned into her, his voice a husky murmur in her ear. "Just so we understand one another." He placed a soft kiss on her temple. "It's not you."

Shaken, Cat pulled her hand away, and this time he let her.

Okay. It definitely wasn't her.

As that knowledge sank in, she began to experience the same intoxicating sensation she'd felt earlier posing in front of the mirror. The power of her feminine appeal.

This man desired her. His body craved her. It was his mind that was putting up roadblocks. She supposed in his own way he was as uncomfortable with this whole situation as she was. He needed to be made to feel like the—what did he call it? The initiator.

What would Delilah do?

Cat shifted into a comfortable cross-legged position, trying to project a nonchalance she didn't feel. "I have to admit, in a way, your decision's a relief," she said, reaching back with both hands to lift her hair off her neck, as she'd practiced in front of the mirror, wishing there was enough light for Greg to appreciate the total effect. "Gosh, is it ever hot in here."

"Yeah, it is. Why?"

"Why what?"

"Why is it a relief? Us not..." He made some sort of hand motion, which she suspected was just crude enough to make her glad she couldn't see it.

She shrugged and leaned back on her palms. "You know—all the pressure of an arrangement like this, the lack of spontaneity."

"I know."

"I mean, talk about sex by the numbers."

"Yeah."

"When we both know you're not into it."

"Right."

"And chances are, I wouldn't even get aroused."

Silence.

"So it's a big relief," she said. "I think there's a pint of Häagen-Dazs melting in the freezer. You want to split it?"

"No. That wouldn't be a problem," he said stiffly.

"What wouldn't be a problem?"

"My being able to get you aroused. No reason to assume that would be a problem. If we were going to do it."

"Which we aren't."

"Right."

"So we'll never really know for sure, but that's neither here nor there. I think it's mocha chocolate chip and I'm not going to let it go to waste." She scooted around him to the edge of the bed.

His voice held no trace of a smile. "We do

know for sure. *I* know for sure, all right? It wouldn't be a problem." His hand bumped her as he spread his arms. "Trust me on this."

"Sure." Rising, she muttered under her breath, "If you say so."

He grabbed her arm as he came to his feet. He was as tall as she remembered. Taller. "What was that?"

"What?"

"What you just said."

"I said, 'sure.'"

"You said, 'if you say so.' I heard you."

"So why are you asking what I said if you heard me? Do you mind?" she said, tugging on her arm.

He didn't let go. "You don't think I could do it. You don't think I could turn you on."

She pasted on a patient smile, knowing he'd hear it in her voice. "Listen. Whether you could or whether you couldn't isn't really relevant, is it? We're both relieved to have the pressure off. I'd just like to relax with a bowl of ice cream. If that's all right with you?"

He dropped her arm. "So that's it, then. You aren't even curious."

Her prolonged exhalation was as eloquent as the words that followed. "You know what? Actually, I know you could do it." She patted his arm, inching in the direction of the ice cream. "There's not a doubt in my mind."

Cat didn't need light to know Greg was gaping in indignation at this blatant attempt to assuage his fragile masculine ego. Outrage rolled off him in waves. But all she heard in his voice was fierce determination as he growled, "Just for the record," and pulled her into his arms.

His mouth seized hers as his strong fingers splayed over her scalp to hold her still. His other arm banded around her back, crushing her to him. His heat, the scent of his skin, the repressed power in his big, hard body, all went to her head in a dizzying blitz.

Greg kissed her with an intensity that left her reeling. Coaxing her mouth open, he touched his tongue to her lips, her teeth, laying claim without actually penetrating. He was teasing her, she knew he was, forcing a response. She resisted, whimpering with the effort.

Even though this was what she'd wanted, to goad him into action, she was overwhelmed; she'd never been kissed like this. There was no question that Greg was in complete control. She felt like Dr. Frankenstein, at the mercy of the beast she'd created.

His hand slid from her back to her bottom. He caressed her through the silk, testing her shape, lightly squeezing her. The excess of sensation was too much; her self-control vaporized. She clung to him, greedily returning his kiss, drawing his tongue into her mouth.

Cat heard Greg's little grunt of satisfaction, and she didn't care. She didn't care that he was just trying to prove a point. Her hunger was a rapacious thing, clawing at her from within. She knew only that she needed this—this and more. More of his mouth commanding hers, more of his touch, unapologetically bold as his hands roamed over her in leisurely perusal.

He ended the kiss but didn't move away, his moist lips a hairbreadth from hers. Their breath mingled in rapid bursts. She looked up, straining her vision, and was rewarded by her first glimpse of his eyes, midnight black and bottomless. Liquid obsidian.

Cat felt a flicker of unease as she stared into those eyes. In the next heartbeat the reason for her discomfort, if one existed, had slipped away from her, as fleeting as the wingbeat of a moth.

"Have I proved my point?" he asked, sounding more winded than after he'd climbed the twenty-two flights of stairs.

"No." Her voice was as shaky as his. "It was a valiant effort, but..." She shrugged.

"It's not nice to fib. You want to rethink that?" He brushed his knuckles over her aching, erect nipples.

She grasped his wrists, biting back the moan of pleasure that tried to escape. "Nothing to rethink."

"I see. Must be the frigid temperature that did this to you," he said, delicately plucking the stiff peaks that pushed against her thin gown. The pleasure of his touch was so acute it was close to pain. He ignored Cat's efforts to dislodge his hands.

"That's not—that's not definitive proof of anything," she said.

"Ah. We insist on definitive proof, do we? The scientific method and all that."

When one large hand slid down her torso, she was ready with an evasive maneuver. He captured both her wrists in one hand and easily held them while he caressed her belly, toying with her sensitive navel until she squirmed.

"Why can't you just admit I'm right?" he asked.

When she said nothing, he slid his hand lower, directly between her legs. Cat stopped breathing. The heat and pressure of his hand were maddening.

"If I touched you here, what would I find?" he murmured, lightly fondling her. "Are you wet?"

His voice had a wicked edge to it. He was enjoying tormenting her. Arrogant man.

"You mean you'd take my word for it? Not very scientific." She parted her legs slightly.

Greg remained motionless for a few heart-stopping seconds, as if considering her wordless invitation. Then his grip tightened on her wrists as his other hand found the hip-high slit in her gown. He drew the material aside.

Cat gasped at his first probing touch; she was beyond wet, beyond ready. She knew the guttural moan that erupted from Greg had nothing to do with triumph at having proved his point. It was an instinctive response, primitive and purely male.

As he deepened his exploration, her mouth opened on a silent cry. Never in her life had she been this aroused. One long finger pushed into her, slowly, and her knees threatened to collapse. He released her wrists and wrapped his arm around her back, supporting her. She grabbed handfuls of his black T-shirt and hung on for dear life as her hips mimicked the hypnotic rhythm of his thrusting finger. Within moments her climax beckoned, just out of reach.

Greg withdrew his hand. Cat failed to restrain a sob of frustration. He trembled slightly as he set her away from him.

Why did he resist it? she wondered. At this point what did it matter who had initiated what? Could his masculine pride be that frail?

She heard his labored breathing, sensed his battle to bring himself under control.

Oh no, you don't, she thought. *Tonight I'm Delilah, and you're mine.*

His voice was gruff. "I'm going to sleep on the sofa."

Cat reached for the bow closing the front of her gown and released it. She loosened the silk cord and let the bodice slip off her shoulders, leaving her bare to the waist. She experienced a moment of dismay as her breasts, freed from the pneumatic enhancement of the tight gown, settled into their natural contours.

Without giving herself time to reconsider, she closed the distance between them, lifted Greg's hand and placed it on her breast. Her apprehension proved ill founded. As much as he'd admired the outrageous negligee, he obviously appreciated the real her even more. His other hand came up and he caressed her with painstaking thoroughness, as if committing every detail to memory: the weight, the shape, the texture of her. His fingers were slightly callused.

Emboldened by a sexual confidence she'd never felt before, Cat wriggled out of the negligee, letting it slide off her hips to puddle on the carpet. She reached for his erection and stroked it through his jeans. Greg's breath caught. He was even harder than before, if that was possible.

"I don't know where you came up with this 'Me Tarzan' nonsense," she said, "but it's getting tiresome. Take off your clothes."

"No."

Her hand froze in midfondle.

He said, "You do it for me."

Cat smiled in the dark. Greg may have won the battle, but there was no doubt in her mind who won the war.

As she worked on his belt buckle, Greg's hands glided up her arms to her shoulders. He dropped soft kisses on her forehead, along the hairline. One hand slipped to her nape and traced the curve of her spine all the way down, making her shiver.

Cat tugged his T-shirt up and he obligingly lifted his arms so she could pull it off. She tossed it aside and placed her palms on his chest, dragging her nails through crisp hair blanketing a wall of solid muscle. Following the narrowing path of hair down his flat belly to the fly of his jeans, she pulled the zipper tab, while nuzzling his corded neck. His hands tangled in her hair as he tipped his head back in mute encouragement.

She hooked her thumbs in his jeans and briefs and pushed them down his long legs. Impatiently he yanked off his sneakers and socks, and kicked away the last of his clothes.

Greg wasted no time backing Cat against the bed. He fell with her onto it and hauled her into the middle. Brusquely he parted her legs, lifted her hips—a rampant, phantasmic demon lover looming over her, unseen.

The strange apprehension she'd felt earlier, when she'd stared into his eyes, returned with a jolt. But there was no time for second thoughts as Greg flexed his hips and pushed into her.

Cat gasped at the stabbing pressure; her nails gouged his arms. Greg went still, clearly struggling to rein himself in.

"Slow," she whispered, wondering if he remembered what she'd told him on the phone, that she hadn't made love in years. She reached up and touched his face, felt the frown lines and the tension as he held himself in check. "Just a little slower," she said. "It's been a long time for me."

Her words seemed to catch him off guard. He started to pull back, started to say something, but the ache had eased and she moved her hips, and whatever he'd wanted to say died on a sharp exhalation.

"Yes," she breathed, as he sank into her and her body welcomed him, clutched greedily at him. "Oh, yes..."

They receded, came together, and Cat cried out in pure carnal bliss. Had it ever been like this for her? Had she ever felt this stark, stunning pleasure, the overwhelming wonder of it?

No. She would have remembered. *This*, she would have remembered.

Cat clawed at Greg's hard waist, feeling the muscles bunch with each powerful thrust. She didn't recognize herself; she'd never met this thrashing, panting woman, never heard herself utter the blunt words that escaped her now—entreaties, imprecations.

Their bodies slid against each other, slippery with sweat. Greg grabbed the headboard for purchase; the fingers of his other hand dug into her hip. Her body wound tighter with each jackhammer thrust until her climax crested like a wave.

"*Greg!*" she screamed, and held fast to him as the wave crashed, dragging her tumbling out of herself.

He gripped her tighter, groaning, plunging hard and deep, lost now in his own sprinting finish. Cat felt his pumping release, the hot jet of life deep within.

She lay beneath him, spent, stroking his sweat-slick back. Sluggishly he started to lift his weight off her, but she quashed the gentlemanly impulse by pulling him back down—earning his gratitude, if she interpreted his drowsy little grunt correctly.

It's done, Cat mused. *I could be a mother in nine months.* The thought of a baby, *her* baby, in her arms, at her breast, was so breathtaking, so immense, her chest ached with it. Her eyes stung with it.

With trembling fingers she touched Greg's face, rendered slack and almost innocent by postcoital inertia. "Thank you," she whispered. "Thank you."

"DON'T YELL AT ME, I know I'm late," Cat said as she scooted into her favorite booth at the Magnolia Coffee Shop.

The good news was the blackout had ended sometime in the middle of the night. The bad news was she'd woken up alone. Which the rational part of her, the part that dreaded the thought of messy entanglements, recognized as a good thing.

While another, insidious little corner of her soul wondered how it would feel to stare into those midnight eyes over cornflakes and coffee. Every morning.

"Well, aren't you the chipper one," Brigit said, as the waitress plunked a cut grapefruit half in front of her. "Must've gotten a good night's sleep."

"Oh yeah." Cat grinned. "Slept like the dead. Ha ha ha."

Brigit regarded her quizzically. Darlene, the waitress, poured a cup of coffee for Cat, asked, "Waffle for you, right?" and sauntered away when she nodded.

"What's with the grapefruit and clear tea?" Cat asked. "You can't stand either one."

"It's back in, the grapefruit diet. The acid burns away fat." At Cat's snort of derision, Brigit added, "Or something like that. Listen, Greg asked me to apologize for him. He knows how frustrated you must be after last night."

Cat choked on her first sip of coffee. "Frustrated? He said that? 'Frustrated'?"

"I know, understatement of the year. Men!" Brigit hacked at her grapefruit, her nose wrinkling in distaste.

If Greg thought he'd left Cat frustrated, he hadn't been paying very close attention!

"Listen, I don't know what he told you," Cat said, with a silky smile, "but this lady is *not* frustrated."

"Semantics." Brigit shrugged, pushing her dark, overlong bangs off her face. "Disappointed, then." She took a bite of grapefruit and forced it down with a grimace.

Cat set down her coffee cup. "Exactly what did he tell you?"

"I told you what he told me. And oh yeah, he hopes he'll get the chance to make it up to you. Ugh, who can eat this stuff?" Brigit tossed her grapefruit spoon on the table. "Darlene!"

"And when did you talk to him, anyway?" Cat demanded.

"Waffle," Brigit called to the waitress. "Extra syrup. Double bacon on the side. And cappuccino—with chocolate shavings."

"Did he call you?" Cat asked. "Did he, like, *report* to you, or what?"

"What're you getting so worked up about? He called me from Boston to let me know his flight had been routed there because of the blackout. He spent the night in Logan Airport and he's still there, waiting for a flight out. Greg never made it to New York."

2

GREG NEVER MADE *it to New York.*

Cat propelled herself through the revolving doors of the midtown office building that housed the agency she worked for and made a beeline for the elevator bank, all on autopilot. Three hours had passed since Brigit had uttered those words, but their impact hadn't lessened. Cat was still in shock.

She'd quickly ascertained that this wasn't some sick joke Brigit was playing on her, that Greg Bannister had indeed not set foot in New York last night, much less climbed twenty-two flights of stairs and made incomparable, no-holds-barred love to her all night. When Cat had managed to find her voice, she'd told Brigit what had happened.

"You're telling me you don't know who you had sex with last night?" Brigit had screeched, as heads swiveled and eyes popped from one end of the Magnolia Coffee Shop to the other.

"Shh! It was dark. How could I know—"

"My God, it could've been anyone!"

"Will you keep your voice down?" Cat had slid as low as her bench seat would allow. "Why didn't you call me at the apartment when you knew Greg wasn't coming?"

"I tried. Couldn't get through."

"But the phone lines shouldn't have been affected by the blackout...except..." She'd sighed. "It's a cordless phone. So there was no power for the base unit."

"Well, that's it, then."

"Oh Lord." Cat had covered her face. "What if I'm pregnant?"

Brigit had pondered that as she tucked in to her waffle. "Well, that would be okay. I mean, isn't that what you want? A guy to do the deed and then get lost?"

Cat leveled a sardonic look at her friend. "I wanted uninvolved, not anonymous. I don't know anything about this man. I don't even know his name."

"Greg should get into town later today. Do you want him to—"

"No!" Cat couldn't sleep with Greg before she found out whether she was pregnant. The only thing worse than knowing a stranger had fathered her child would be not knowing *which* stranger had fathered her child.

Now, as Cat stepped out of the elevator on the fifth floor, she tried to refocus her thoughts on her work. The double doors marked Office Mom, Inc., stood invitingly open. Nana had summoned her for a one-o'clock meeting, no doubt to review her next assignment. Cat had just completed a two-week gig at a medical insurance company downtown. Nana's office moms were in high demand; they never went more than a day or two between jobs.

Her stride didn't slow as she passed Nana's

assistant, Amory, in the outer office. "Nice tie, Ame. Did it come with 3-D glasses?"

Amory smirked. Cat gave him no end of grief over his ugly neckties. "She's waiting for you."

She waggled her fingers in acknowledgment and sailed into Nana's office with a perfunctory knock. Cat's employer sat behind her leather-topped, antique French desk, or *bureau plat*, as she called it. Her shrimp pink bouclé suit was adorned with a round, pearl-studded brooch. Short silver hair framed her face in a simple, elegant style. As always, the scent of Joy perfume lingered in the air.

"Here's our Caitlin now!" Nana announced, with a warm smile. She gestured to the seating area in front of her desk. "Dear, I'd like you to meet Mr. Mikhailov."

Cat turned toward the man now rising from his chair. Her hand was outstretched, a polite smile firmly in place.

"Brody," he said, and enveloped her fingers in a firm handshake.

In the next heartbeat the vague sense of recognition congealed into an iron ball in her stomach. Cat froze with her hand in his, stupefied. She watched Brody Mikhailov's genial smile falter as he sensed her turmoil, watched the reason for it install itself in his consciousness.

It was all the same. The deep, mellifluous voice…the inviting scent of his skin…the bristly shadow of beard stubble that had gently chafed her throat, her breasts, the insides of her thighs, not twelve hours ago.

Cat looked into his eyes. *Those* eyes. They

weren't black, after all, she now realized, but inky indigo blue.

She stood mute, numb, her synapses on overload. After an initial flash of surprise, Brody's expression gave nothing away, even as the awesome truth crackled between them like heat lightning.

Nana's voice held concern. "Caitlin?"

My job. What's going to happen to my job?

Cat tried to force a response past her constricted throat. Brody gave her hand a little squeeze. He steered her away from Nana and toward the guest chairs.

"It's the heat out there, Mrs. Littlestone," he said. "I saw a traffic cop keel over on Third." For Cat's ears only he murmured, "You're doing fine. Take a deep breath."

He settled her in the seat he'd just vacated, one of a pair of low-backed Bergère chairs upholstered in champagne-colored jacquard silk. She filled her lungs as ordered and exhaled slowly.

Nana half rose. "You're pale."

"I'll be fine," Cat said, her voice wobbly. "Mr.—Mr. Mikhailov is right. It's the heat. I—I walked from, um…I had to park across town."

Nana lowered herself into her chair, her expression mildly reproving. "Do use one of the parking garages nearby, dear, when the weather's extreme. Submit the receipts to Amory."

"Thank you, Nana, I will." Cat avoided looking at Brody as he dropped into the chair next to hers.

"'Nana'?" he said. "Is Caitlin your…no, that's impossible. If you have grandchildren, Mrs. Littlestone, they must be infants."

Cat had never before seen her employer blush, but now her color rose to match her pink outfit.

"It's a nickname I acquired some years ago," Nana explained. "As a matter of fact, I recently became a great-grandmother. No no." She raised a hand, forestalling his next comment. "If you dish out any more outlandish flattery, I might start believing it."

As she sat listening to this vapid exchange, Cat's initial stupor began to give way to dread. There could be only one reason for this meeting. Thinking fast, she opened her mouth to speak, only to be preempted by her boss.

"Once the lights went out last night, Mr. Mikhailov, I'm sure you wished I'd never offered you use of the agency's apartment. It must have been wretchedly uncomfortable."

"Not at all."

Did Cat only imagine the suggestive undertone in Brody's voice? She sneaked a peek at him, just as his devilish gaze homed in on her.

"Last night turned out to be a rare and remarkable experience," he said. "A matter of finding myself in the right place at the right time, you might say."

"Well, of course, the view from the terrace must have been extraordinary. I'm relieved you're able to look on the bright side of the blackout." Nana tittered. "So to speak."

"Oh. Let me give these back to you." Brody

fished a pair of keys out of his pocket and leaned forward to place them on Nana's desk. "Thanks again."

That morning Cat had wondered why Greg had returned the keys to their hiding spot under the apartment's doormat when he left. Now she realized they'd been there all night.

"I still haven't located that second set," Nana fretted as she dropped the keys in a side drawer of her desk. "I can't imagine where they might have gotten to."

Brody looked at Cat again, his expression outwardly neutral. Except that his level stare was just a tad too blunt. And that sensual mouth, which had given her so much pleasure last night, now quirked up at one corner, mockingly. If he chose to, he could tell Nana who had swiped the other set of keys.

Cat sent him a wordless plea. *Don't do it. Please. I need this job.*

Without taking his eyes off her, Brody said, "This wasn't my idea." The words gave her a jolt. Hadn't he said the same thing last night, when he'd tried to rebuff her?

What on earth did he think she'd been doing there, anyway, in the agency's apartment, which Nana had lent him for the night? She must have appeared to be lying in wait for him—in that obscene nightgown! Forget about conversation, she'd told him, forget about foreplay. Let's just get down to it.

Good Lord! What did he think—that she was some closet nymphomaniac intent on seducing her employer's clients?

Cat struggled to uphold her end of the conversation. "What…what do you mean, not your idea?"

Brody slouched indolently in the chair and crossed his legs, ankle over knee. "You're my fortieth-birthday present."

"Excuse me?"

"My agent, Leon Lopez, thought it would do me good to have an office mom hanging around for a month. How did Leon put it? A little TLC might have a humanizing effect on me." Brody wagged his finger at her. "Something tells me a month of your particular brand of TLC will leave me feeling like a new man, Caitlin."

There was that breezy grin again. The corners of his eyes bore permanent creases. *I was right*, Cat thought. This man spent a lot of time smiling.

"Your instincts are correct, Mr. Mikhailov," Nana said. "Caitlin is our most popular nurturer. The clients she works with almost always request her services again."

"That doesn't surprise me in the least," Brody said. "And speaking from personal experience, if I don't get *nurtured* on a regular basis, I get cranky as hell."

So that was it. Nana's newest client was looking forward to a month of the kind of "nurturing" he'd received last night. Perhaps he thought it was a free sample to drum up business!

Nana said, "The office mom philosophy is rather unique, Mr. Mikhailov. Did you by any chance peruse the brochure I gave you yesterday?"

"Oh heck. And I'll bet there's gonna be a pop quiz."

Nana smiled indulgently. "Since you've never used our services before, please bear with me for a few moments. It may prevent some confusion down the road. The concept of the office mom was conceived as a response to the depersonalization inherent in the modern American business milieu. Office workers nowadays must cope with a rigid hierarchy, divisive office politics and a soulless physical environment, be it a posh corner office with a view or some lonely little cubicle in a sea of lonely little cubicles. Are you with me so far, Mr. Mikhailov?"

"Like a rash."

"An office mom will join a company as a sort of temporary employee, or consultant, if you will. She lavishes tender loving care on the workers, the kind of attention an actual mother might bestow."

"Mercy. I'd better be good or Caitlin'll send me to bed without my supper."

Nana answered this with a tolerant smile. If Cat had a dollar for every time she'd heard that lame remark or some variation thereof, she wouldn't have to worry about losing her job.

"Seriously," Brody said. "What kind of mommy stuff are we talking about here? Sewing a button on my shirt? Milk and cookies in the afternoon?"

"If you'd like," Nana said. "Whatever it takes to make one feel cared for and comforted. It's important that the client understands, too, what an office mom is *not*. While she may perform the occasional light chore or errand, and, of course, prepare your milk and cookies—" she flashed a brisk little smile "—she is not a housekeeper, cook, baby-sitter or nurse. And I'm certain it goes without saying that excessive familiarity will not be tolerated. Office Mom, Inc., is not a dating or escort service."

"What if she makes the first move?" Brody gave Cat an exaggerated wink.

Her heart stuttered. *Don't even kid about this!* she wanted to scream. *Nana must never know!*

"In that case we have absolutely nothing to worry about," Nana stated confidently. "Caitlin is a professional. I know she'd never breach my trust in such a manner."

Cat dropped her gaze to her lap and smoothed an invisible wrinkle from her calf-length floral chiffon skirt.

"Of course she wouldn't," Brody said. "When can she start?"

"She can't," Cat blurted.

They looked at her.

"I...I can't work with Mr. Mikhailov. My, um, schedule...I have commitments. For the next month."

Nana blinked. "Commitments? I don't recall assigning—"

"Not an assignment. It's personal. I'm...going on vacation. I guess I, uh, forgot to mention it to you."

Though Nana schooled her expression well, Cat read both annoyance and surprise. In seven years working for the agency, Cat had always been the model of dependability.

Cat said, "Why don't you let Rhonda be Mr. Mikhailov's office mom? She's free at the moment, isn't she?" Rhonda had the added advantage of looking like a clean-shaven Willie Nelson.

"I don't know," Brody said, "I've kind of got my heart set on Caitlin here."

There it was again. That indigo stare. Too direct. Too eloquent. Cat forced herself to meet it without flinching.

"Unfortunately, I'm not available," she said evenly. "I'm sure Rhonda will suit—"

"You see, the thing is…" Brody broke eye contact with Cat and turned to Nana "…if I can't have Caitlin, I'm not interested."

Nana said, "But—but Mr. Lopez already arranged—"

Brody shrugged. "Guess you'll just have to refund Leon's money. He'll buy me a watch. It's Caitlin or no one. You said yourself, she's the best."

"Well. We appear to be at something of an impasse." Nana turned to Cat. "Just how firm are these vacation plans, dear?" Her eyebrows rose fractionally, prompting the answer she expected to hear from her most reliable employee.

Before Cat could say, *Pretty darn firm*, Brody jumped in.

"So. Caitlin. Where were *you* when the lights went out?"

Cat's gaze snapped to his. Beneath his affable expression she detected a cold ruthlessness.

Nana answered for her. "Caitlin has a lovely little place in Westchester, so the blackout didn't affect her. Isn't that right, dear?"

"Um…yes."

Brody never took his eyes off Cat. He shifted toward her, propped his elbow on the arm of the chair and absently scratched his bristly chin. "When Nana gave me the keys yesterday, she couldn't find the second set—someone must've borrowed them. So when I got to the apartment last night, I half expected to find myself with a roommate. One of Nana's lovely office moms, perhaps, sleeping as peacefully as Goldilocks."

Cat clenched the chair arms so hard her fingers cramped. Her strained chuckle sounded more like a wheeze. "That's some imagination you've got. Hope you weren't too disappointed to find yourself all alone."

He didn't respond, but studied her wordlessly for a few moments, still with that damn amiable expression. Cat's pulse whooshed in her ears. She swallowed a hard, dry lump of dread. Finally she had to look away.

He'd do it. He'd tell Nana. He'd tell her about the purloined keys. The naughty negligee. All that "hold the foreplay and take off your clothes, Tarzan" stuff. Cat could deny it, of course, but she was a pitifully inept liar. And it wouldn't simply be her word against his. All Nana would have to do was ask the doorman if anyone other than Brody had used the apartment last night, and Cat would be busted.

"But I interrupted," Brody said. "My apologies. Nana was asking you about your vacation plans."

Cat licked her dry lips. She looked at her employer. "It's nothing I can't postpone. I'll be happy to be Mr. Mikhailov's office mom. I can start on Monday."

3

SPOT SET UP a hellacious howl downstairs, barking and snarling at the front door. Brody scanned the computer room for the cheap digital clock Leon had bought him. There it was, precariously perched on a heap of paperbacks that were themselves precariously perched on top of the computer monitor. Twelve noon on the button. She was punctual.

Brody abhorred punctuality. He took a last drag of his cigarette and ground the butt in the ashtray balanced on his knee, a weighty slab of green glass he'd swiped from a steak pub during his misspent youth. He thumbed the red buttons on his handheld electronic game a half dozen more times, annihilating two giant lizard warriors and a grenade-chucking alien octopus, to the accompaniment of staccato bursts of static from his Gatling gun.

Brody shoved himself out of the frilly, chintz-covered wing chair, deposited the toy and the ashtray on the empty pizza box on the floor and headed down the hall to the stairs as the doorbell rang. He had to keep to the banister side of the stairway, because the wall side was piled high with newspapers, magazines and all manner of household items waiting to be carted either upstairs or down.

"You tell 'er, Spot!" Brody hollered, goading the big old mutt into canine hysteria. "Don't you let her get away with that! You tell her, boy! You tell her who's boss!" He patted the shaggy black fur, rubbed the animal's frosted muzzle.

Brody opened the door to the enclosed wraparound porch, which stretched across the front of the house and down one side. Spot pushed past him, still doing his vicious-watchdog imitation. The doorbell rang again. Brody grabbed hold of Spot's collar and opened the front door.

He almost didn't recognize her. That magnificent red hair was pulled back in a severe French twist. In contrast to the flattering, feminine outfit she'd worn in Nana's office, she was now dressed in a crisp white shirt, tailored navy blue jacket with matching knee-length skirt, and practical pumps. She carried a boxy briefcase of polished black leather. Impenetrable sunglasses concealed her eyes.

"Nice look, babe," Brody said. "I'm feeling nurtured already."

Caitlin took a step back.

"Don't worry," he said. "At his age, Spot's bark is, I'm sad to say, worse than his bite. Settle down now, boy."

"I'm not concerned about the dog. Couldn't you have thrown something on to answer the door?"

Brody glanced down at his snug white B.V.D.s. "I did."

She scowled.

"Come on, Caitlin. After the other night...?" He snapped the elastic waistband of his briefs. "You're kidding, right?"

"If you can't even try to maintain a dignified atmosphere—"

"I thought you office moms rejected the soulless, repressive, Brave New World trappings of modern business."

"Like clothes?"

"Listen, let's take this conversation inside." He yanked her by the arm. "Before my neighbors decide I'm being kidnapped by one of the Blues Sisters."

Caitlin could deck herself out head to toe in a suit of armor, but she couldn't touch his memories. Brody had no trouble picturing her as she'd been that night, eagerly seductive, baring her lush body, brazenly offering herself—and demanding that he take what she offered. All of which had seemed consistent with who he'd thought she was and what he'd thought she was doing there.

Until he'd encountered her again in Nana's office and realized his mistake. Now he had a few questions for his oh-so-proper office mom.

Caitlin removed her sunglasses as she passed through the porch, staring at her surroundings with an awestruck expression. Cartons of files were stacked three deep. White wicker furniture groaned under memorabilia amassed during research trips spanning the last two decades. A couple of dozen free-standing metal shelving units were crammed with hundreds—no, make

that thousands—of books. Brody had never gotten rid of a book in his life.

"Good grief," she murmured. "What a fire
hazard!"

She followed Brody into the living room. He
released Spot, who proceeded to treat their visitor to a more intimate sniff-and-slobber welcome. She backed away, nearly upsetting the
televisions.

"That's enough of that." Brody hauled the
dog off Caitlin. "She's not your type, Spot. Too
preppy. You're more of a polyester kind of guy.
You wanna go out? Wanna go out?"

This, of course, was the doggie equivalent of
"You just won the lottery." Spot answered with
a sharp, gleeful yip and trotted toward the
kitchen and the back door as fast as his arthritic
hips would allow.

Brody let him out and returned to the living
room to find Caitlin examining the tower of four
TVs she'd nearly knocked over. It was more of a
pyramid, really, with the twenty-seven-incher,
the only one that worked, on the floor and the
ancient thirteen-inch black-and-white on the
top. She said, "I'm not going to ask."

"Great. Let me show you the office."

"Put something on first."

"I wish you'd give this old-maid routine a
rest. I just got out of the shower, okay?" He
started up the stairs, not looking to see whether
she followed. After a moment he heard her disgruntled voice behind him.

"I didn't know this was a *home* office until I

got here. What kind of work do you do, Mr. Mikhailov?"

Brody stopped and grinned at her over his shoulder. She nearly bumped into him. "'Mr. Mikhailov'?"

He waited. She sighed. "Brody."

He took the remaining steps two at a time. "I'm a writer."

"Oh. What do you write?"

The upstairs was bisected by a long center hall. Brody stepped into the first room on the right, the largest, and grabbed a pair of jeans off the peach-on-peach-striped chaise longue, piled high with clean laundry. The only area free of work-related clutter was the sleeping alcove, which housed the old-fashioned four-poster bed.

"Oh my God," Caitlin breathed. "You're married." She stood in the doorway, gaping at the peach sprigged wallpaper and ruffled lace curtains. "I had s—" She covered her mouth with her hand.

She didn't finish the sentence. She didn't have to. *I had sex with a married man.*

Brody chewed back a wry smile as he stepped into his jeans and zipped up. "No, you didn't," he said. "I'm not married. Never have been."

Caitlin stared at him a moment. Her gaze flicked over the ultrafeminine furnishings.

"The place came like this," he said.

"Oh."

"Buddy of mine got the house in his divorce settlement. He didn't want it, was moving to

Montreal, sold it to me. It was his ex-wife who fixed it up like this."

"How long have you been here?"

"Four years."

"Four years? And you haven't redecorated?"

He shrugged. "I don't much notice what the place looks like anymore."

"No kidding," she muttered, hastily stepping aside as he exited the room. He knew her comment had more to do with clutter than decor.

She trailed him down the hall. "Aren't you going to put on a shirt? Or shoes?"

"It's hot. How can you stand that jacket?"

"I assumed you'd have air-conditioning."

"Don't care for it." He paused at the next doorway. "This is the computer room. It's where I do most of my work."

Her eyes lit on the pizza box, the cardboard cartons overflowing with reference books, the mountain of yellowing newspapers, the piles of rubber-band-bound manuscripts, accumulated over nineteen years, the empty coffee cups and shot glasses. Her gaze lingered on the empty bottle of Russian vodka. "Uh-huh."

He moved on. "That's the john," he said, pointing to the end-of-hall bathroom and stopping at the doorway of the room opposite the computer room. Inside was a Universal machine, free weights, a stereo system and more books, hardcover and paperback, piled on shelves and stacked on the floor. "Workout room slash music room slash library."

"If this is your library, what are all those books on the porch?" she asked.

"Those are like the archives down there. This is more current stuff. That pile there is TBR." At her quizzical look he said, "To be read."

She took a deep breath. "Listen. I'd assumed that you had a, you know, a regular office. With employees?"

He spread his arms. "What you see is what you get."

"You still haven't told me what you write."

"You've probably read some of it." He stepped over a pile of compact discs, plucked a handful of paperbacks off a shelf and tossed one to her. She caught it and looked at the cover. Her eyes grew huge. He handed her the others.

"You write *these?*" Her features twisted into a grimace.

This wasn't the first time his work had provoked such a response, but it was the first time in memory that it had bothered him. "It's a dirty job, but someone's gotta do it."

She shoved the books into his hands as if fearing contamination. "Why?"

"Because people want to read it. The public has an insatiable appetite for information about celebrities."

"'Information'? Don't you mean gossip? Unsubstantiated rumors? *Lies?*"

"I do my research."

Her sardonic look spoke volumes.

He said, "You can count on getting more accurate information from unauthorized biographies than from authorized ones." Why was he getting into this with her? He thought he'd transcended the need to defend himself years ago.

"'Unauthorized biographies,'" she said. "That almost makes it sound legitimate. If you're so proud of what you write, why hide behind a pen name?"

"Back when I was starting out, my agent thought a name like Mikhailov might turn off American readers. He's the one who came up with 'Jake Beckett.' And I've never hid behind the damn pseudonym. It's not like I'm trying to conceal my identity." He spread his arms. "If someone doesn't like what I write about them, let 'em sue me." He'd dodged that bullet more than once.

Caitlin tapped one of the paperbacks he held, the cover of which featured an unflattering photograph of a well-known aging starlet. "Well, I don't think you have to worry about Serena suing you."

That was true. Serena Milton had overdosed on barbiturates within days after Brody's *Serena!* hit the bookstores. After her death, sales of the book skyrocketed; it went to four printings. Brody wondered if he'd ever stop thinking of those royalties as blood money.

The bottom line was, he'd never know what role his tell-all book had played in Serena's suicide. He told himself she'd been close to the edge anyway, living her own private hell of emotional instability, destructive relationships, career burnout and financial ruin. If he hadn't jumped at the opportunity to make that private hell public, someone else would have beat him to it.

That was what he told himself, but it was cold

comfort when he lay awake in the middle of the night picturing that grainy morgue snapshot of Serena that had somehow found its way onto the cover of one of those supermarket tabloids.

Brody had no intention of sharing his personal torment with anyone, much less this sanctimonious "nurturer." He despised Caitlin's smug judgmentalism, despised himself for letting it get to him. He tossed the books on the floor and strode down the hall to the last door, opposite his bedroom.

"If you haven't figured it out yet, my office is basically the whole upstairs."

Caitlin peered through the open doorway. "Another computer room?"

"Oh, that's an old machine," he said, referring to the 386 PC incongruously perched on the elegant dressing table. A host of other obsolete and nonfunctional gadgets were heaped on the lowboy dresser and the canopied guest bed: lamps, radios, toaster ovens, blenders, a microwave, stereo turntable, VCR, fax machine, manual typewriter, electric typewriter, electronic typewriter, dedicated word processor, daisy-wheel printer, dot-matrix printer, ink-jet printer, laser printer and a first-generation game-playing computer.

"Why are you keeping all these things?" she asked.

"I'm going to fix 'em. When I get the chance."

"Ha ha ha."

"Not all of this stuff is broken," he said. "Some of it I've replaced with newer models, but there's no point in just throwing it away.

Maybe someone can use it." He indicated the photocopy machine in the corner, on which sat an ancient slide projector. "That copier works."

"Doesn't look like it gets much use."

"It just needs toner."

"How long has it needed toner?"

"Let me show you the kitchen. Have you had breakfast?"

"Five hours ago. What's in the garbage bags?" she asked, pointing to the dozen or so dark green overstuffed leaf bags next to the bed.

"Garbage."

He figured he'd better get used to that grimace.

"Not my garbage," he clarified. "Other people's."

She stared at him. "Is this something else I really don't want to know about?"

"I would say so, yes."

"Oh, wait a minute. This isn't…you don't go through their trash, do you? The people you write about?"

"Hey, it's not stealing. It's right there on the curb, for anyone to help themselves to. You know, that particular expression is not your most attractive look."

She threw her hands up. "This situation is impossible, Brody. I can't work with you."

"Would it help if I told you it's all bills and receipts and correspondence in those bags, nothing icky?"

"I'm not talking about the garbage. I'm talking about us. You know as well as I do this is just…it's just *impossible*."

"Why?"

"*Why*? After what happened between us?"

Brody grinned. He crossed his arms over his bare chest and leaned a shoulder on the doorframe. "Now, I know what I said in Nana's office, but I didn't actually go up to that apartment the other night expecting to find Goldilocks in a naughty nightie. 'What happened between us,' as you so coyly put it, wasn't—"

"I know," she muttered. "It wasn't your idea. And you'd be more than happy to inform my employer whose idea it was."

"Indeed I would. And no doubt she'd ask the same question that's been plaguing me. Why?"

He waited for her to satisfy his curiosity. Why had she been in that apartment? What had prompted that outrageous seduction?

Finally she grumbled, "Can I get something cold to drink?"

"Follow me."

In the kitchen Caitlin dropped her briefcase, stripped off her jacket and tossed it on a chairback. She unbuttoned her cuffs and rolled up her sleeves, unpinned the simple brooch at her throat and loosened her collar.

"Beer?" Brody opened the refrigerator.

"Water." She flopped into a wicker-seated Breuer chair and rested her elbows on the blond oak table. "Okay. It's like this. I have this boyfriend. Greg Bannister. He lives in Alaska."

"Alaska." He dropped a few ice cubes in a tumbler. "Does Greg in Alaska know how you entertain yourself during blackouts in New York?"

"Well, see, that's the thing. It's funny really. What happened. Kind of a comedy of errors."

He filled the tumbler with water and handed it to her. "I could use a giggle."

"Okay, well…Greg and I, we met three years ago, right before he moved to Alaska. He's my friend Brigit's cousin and…and she introduced us and, well, I guess we hit it off." She took a sip of water. "I mean, we didn't do anything about it then, you know, but after he left, we corresponded. E-mailed each other every day."

"Let me guess. You bared your soul. Discovered a kindred spirit." He tapped a cigarette out of the pack on the counter and lit up.

"Can I ask you to please not smoke?"

"Yes." He leaned back against the counter, took a long drag and exhaled lazily.

She stared at him. Finally she said, "Would you please not smoke?"

"No. So you and Greg spent the last three years writing dirty E-mail to each other."

Caitlin stiffened. "It wasn't like that. We…we fell in love."

"Gosh. That's just so darn romantic."

His sarcasm jerked her chin up. "Greg is a wonderful man. Sensitive. Intelligent. He has an important, *respectable* career. As an engineer. On the oil pipeline."

"Mr. Perfect."

"Anyway, a few days ago he told me he was coming to New York. We…we arranged to meet, to, um…you know."

"To consummate this grand passion that had blossomed in cyberspace."

"Yeah."

"In the apartment belonging to the agency you work for."

"Well, yeah. But the problem was, his plane got delayed. Because of the blackout."

"And when I showed up instead of Mr. Perfect, you decided what the heck, one guy's the same as—"

"No! I thought you were Greg."

One look at her sober expression told him it wasn't a joke. "That's ludicrous."

"I know it sounds...but you have to understand. I didn't really know Greg. I mean, I wasn't that familiar with him physically, even though we'd gotten real close emotionally. I just met him the once. And it was dark when you and I..."

"There was a little moonlight. I'm not buying it, Caitlin."

"I...wasn't wearing my contacts. I'm blind without them. I saw *nothing*, Brody. I swear."

He pushed off the counter and leaned over her, peering at her eyes. There, floating on the striking, ice blue irises, were contact lenses. He straightened.

"You do look like him," she said. "I mean, the resemblance is startling."

"My voice...?" he said.

"Greg and I didn't really speak on the phone. Too expensive. We stuck to E-mail." She shrugged. "You, uh, sound kind of like him, too."

Brody turned away to think it through. Was it possible? He recalled how stunned she'd been when they'd met in Nana's office—scant hours after "Greg" had left her asleep, without so much as a so-long-it-was-fun note. The pieces fit even before he remembered.

He faced her. "You called me Greg."

"I did? Why didn't you say something?"

"I was distracted." He smiled grimly. "So were you, at the time."

He watched comprehension dawn. Watched a wave of crimson crawl up her face.

"I—I'm—" she stammered.

"Don't apologize. You thought I was Mr. Perfect."

"But you didn't know that then."

"It didn't really bother me that much. I don't believe anyone should be held accountable for what they scream at the height of passion."

She cringed. "I screamed?"

He grinned. "We're talking serious decibels, babe."

"Please don't call me that."

"Yes, Mom." He stubbed out his cigarette.

"You know, that's not funny, Brody, that's tasteless, under the circumstances. It's…eww, I don't know what it is. Call me Cat. Only Nana calls me Caitlin."

"I like that. Cat. Brings to mind all that feline sensuality I recall so vividly. So now I know who you thought I was. You haven't asked me who I thought you were." Brody savored the anticipation. This was going to be fun after hearing about Mr. Perfect.

"Well…I assumed you just thought I was…well, me," she said. "You know. One of

Nana's employees. Someone with access to the—"

He stopped her with a raised palm. "Nana's assistant—Amos, is it?"

"Amory."

"After Nana gave me the keys, Amory took me aside and told me there'd be a surprise waiting for me in the bedroom. When I saw what the surprise was, I figured Leon had to have been in on it as well."

Cat's brow wrinkled. Suddenly she recoiled, wide-eyed. "You thought..."

Brody should have enjoyed her stricken expression. He should have enjoyed seeing her eyes glaze with tears of mortification. Instead he found himself squirming.

"Cat, come on, it's...it's funny. Like with Greg. A comedy of—"

"Is that what you thought?" Blotches of color stained her cheeks. "That I was a...a *prostitute?*"

He sighed. Pushed his fingers through his hair. "Look. I find you waiting for me, in that getup, eager as hell, after being told—"

"There was a basket!" She slapped the table with her open palm. Water sloshed out of her glass.

"What?"

"There was a gourmet food basket! That was the damn surprise! Didn't you see it? There's always a basket waiting for the next guest of the agency." Cat pinched the bridge of her nose.

Brody swore under his breath. He groped for the cigarette pack and gave it a good tap, only to watch half a dozen cigarettes shoot out onto the floor. Squatting to pick them up, he said, "Look, I didn't think you were a street hooker or anything like that. I thought you were an expensive call girl. Real high class."

"Oh, thank you!" She swiped at her eyes before the tears could spill.

He stood, tossed the cigarettes on the counter. "Listen, what do I know from hookers? I've never used one in my life. And I don't intend to, even if someone else is paying. That's why I didn't want to do it. At first."

Brody stood watching Cat, who was hunched miserably over the table, her head in her hands. Now, looking back on it, he marveled that he could have mistaken this woman for an experienced lady of the evening. True, she'd been eager, even impatient, but she'd been nervous, as well—an irresistible blend of innocence and eroticism that had really pushed his buttons. And she'd been tight. Practically virginal.

It's been a long time for me, she'd said, and he'd tried to stop then, demand an explanation. He might as well have tried to stop breathing. He'd never had sex like that. At the time he'd tried to tell himself it was because she was a professional, but even then he'd known that had nothing to do with it. He'd never experienced those physical and emotional peaks, never felt that depth of connection with a woman.

Brody knew Cat desperately wanted out of this assignment, that she couldn't bear the thought of spending the next month working closely with him. He had no intention of granting her wish. The prospect of having this sexy, intriguing woman at his beck and call for an entire month excited him. Maybe he'd even manage to make her forget Mr. Perfect long enough for a repeat performance. If that made him a selfish bastard, so be it.

Brody placed his hand on Cat's shoulder. She flinched. "I have to ask. Were you using birth control?"

Cat tensed under his fingers. Brody held his breath. She uncovered her face and directed her glassy gaze to the tabletop. "Yes. I'm on the Pill."

Brody exhaled gustily. He squeezed her shoulder. "Well, thank God for that."

4

"EXCUSE ME," Cat said, pulling an oven mitt onto her hand. "Those cookies should be ready."

Brody stepped away from the pot boiling on the stove top long enough for her to slide the cookie sheet out of the oven. The mingled aromas of fresh-baked oatmeal cookies and sautéed veal cutlets filled the kitchen. Cat lifted the soft cookies one by one with a spatula and deposited them on a layer of paper towels on the tabletop.

Brody poked a chunk of cooked potato with a fork. "Done."

Spot lay sprawled in the corner on the cool terra-cotta tiles, inches from his luxurious custom-made dog bed. Only his amber eyes moved as he watched his master dump the potatoes into a colander to drain, then return them to the pot and start whaling away at them with the masher.

"Doesn't that dog ever have a yen for Alpo?" Cat asked, having observed the identical ritual for three days running.

"Spot won't touch that slop. Would you?" Brody poured warm milk and melted butter into the potatoes, added a sprinkle of salt and continued mashing.

"No, but I don't lick myself or drink out of toilets either." She set the empty cookie sheet in the sink. "It just seems a little strange. I mean, you don't cook for *yourself*, Brody. But your dog gets this royal treatment."

"This guy's been with me a long time. Since he was a puppy. Loyalty like that deserves to be rewarded. Isn't that right, boy?"

Brody loaded the mashed potatoes onto Spot's special plate and shaped them into an appetizing mound. He placed the veal cutlets on the plate and began cutting them into itty-bitty bite-size pieces, in deference to the animal's sore gums and missing teeth. This was Spot's cue to rouse himself and lumber over to where the action was. He settled on his haunches, licking his chops and sweeping the floor with his tail.

"You're my good buddy, aren't you, boy? You deserve the best, don't you? Sure you do." Brody placed the laden plate by Spot's water bowl. "Besides," he told Cat, "he can't eat that canned stuff anymore. It upsets his stomach." As the dog began to devour his dinner, Brody gave his big head a couple of brisk pats and lovingly ran his hand over the thick black fur.

He took time out every day not just to prepare the geriatric mutt's food, but to walk him and play with him as well. Yesterday he'd bathed him and inspected him for fleas and ticks. The day before, Spot's creaky old hips had clearly been a little achier than usual and Brody had rushed him to the veterinarian.

Cat said, "That animal has got your number," but she couldn't deny there was something touching about the tender care Brody lavished on his old pet.

"Spoken like someone who's never owned a dog," Brody said, with that patented grin.

"I don't know how people have the patience to walk them, or clean up after them. I myself refuse to arrange my day around the bowel habits of a lower life-form."

"No cats? No birds?" He swiped a warm cookie and shoved it whole into his mouth. "Nothing to take care of?"

She resisted the urge to touch her abdomen. "No," she said. "Nothing."

During the week that had elapsed since their bizarre first encounter, Cat had tried not to dwell on the possibility that her initial plan had worked and Brody's seed had taken root in her womb. She wanted a baby, yes, but not by *him*. Ironically, after craving it for so long, scheming for it, she now prayed she wasn't pregnant. Then she could start fresh with someone else— the kind of man she'd originally had in mind. Greg Bannister, if she could reschedule their rendezvous. Even Anton Lind. *Anyone* but Brody Mikhailov, a slovenly, conscienceless scandalmonger with a devastating smile and the sexual stamina of a satyr.

"What are you thinking?" he asked. "What put that glazed look on your face?"

She blinked away the satyric reminiscences. "I was wondering why you named him Spot."

Brody shrugged. "Why not? It's a good solid dog's name. Simple. Unpretentious."

"He doesn't have a spot."

"What?"

"He's all black. Not a spot to be seen. That animal is spot-free."

A sullen glower replaced Brody's cocky grin. "Where's my milk?" he demanded, snatching up his pack of cigarettes. "You're supposed to be fixing me milk and cookies."

"You going to eat and smoke at the same time?"

"Maybe."

She opened the refrigerator and retrieved the carton of milk. Without facing him she said, "Spot, tell your master to stop making faces at me."

Cat turned back with a smug smile, gratified by his how-did-she-know? expression. "I'm a mom, remember? I have eyes in the back of my head." She reached into a cabinet for two glasses and filled them with milk.

Brody started to tuck a cigarette between his lips, but stopped to say, "Are you?" At her questioning look, he added, "A mom. For real."

Quickly she turned back to the cabinet for a plate. "Like you, I've never been married."

"That doesn't answer my question."

Cat kept her eyes on the cookies she was piling onto the plate. "No. I'm not a mom."

"That's a shame."

Her gaze flashed to his face.

"You seem to enjoy your job," he said. "Taking care of people. You're good at it."

She gave a dismissive half laugh. "There's a big difference between playing Donna Reed from nine to five and being responsible for another human being day in and day out."

Instead of "nine to five," Cat should have said "noon to eight," her current office-mom hours, as dictated by Brody, who saw no reason to adhere to a normal work schedule. He devoted sporadic chunks of time to his current writing project, beginning sometime in midafternoon and knocking off around two or three in the morning.

He flung the cigarette onto the counter, unlit, and took the plate from her. She followed him outside, where they took seats across from each other at the glass-topped picnic table shaded by a green-and-white-striped umbrella. Spot trotted across the deep lawn and started nosing around the rhododendrons edging the tall ash fence.

It was hot and sunny, but Cat was comfortable, thanks to a mild breeze and her summery outfit of loden-colored walking shorts, sleeveless white T-shirt and sandals. After the first day, she'd dispensed with the stuffy buttoned-up look she'd wrongly assumed would help establish a professional atmosphere. Nothing about Brody Mikhailov, his place of business or his work habits was even remotely professional. This office-mom gig was more like baby-sitting.

Which sort of made sense, she reflected, since her client was the quintessential Peter Pan—a lost boy refusing to grow up.

"So you don't want kids?" Brody said, dunking a cookie in his milk and leaning back in his chair.

Cat had hoped he'd abandoned this particular conversational thread. "I didn't say that." She forced a light tone. "Maybe someday. You never know what the future holds."

"Ever think of settling down with Mr. Perfect in Alaska?"

"That's really none of your concern, Brody."

He looked across the yard for a moment, to where Spot was sniffing the base of the back fence. He took a long swallow of milk. "I've been wondering about something. That night. When you thought I was Greg."

"I don't want to discuss—"

"Did you think this guy you'd fallen for was rejecting you because you came on so strong in the sex department?"

She stared at him, at a loss for how to respond.

"I mean, once you realized how turned on I was, what did you think when I didn't want to do it?" he said. "Which was because of, you know, who I thought you were at the time, but you didn't know that. What did you think was going through my head? Greg's head?"

"What does it matter?" she said tightly, still mortified at having been mistaken for a prostitute.

"Just curious. You say you love this guy. You must've gotten some kind of insight into his character after three years of lovey-dovey E-mail. Were you surprised when 'Greg' said no? Is he the kind of chest-thumping throwback who's too insecure to let the little lady assert herself sexually?"

"I can't imagine what makes you think you have the right to ask that."

"Never said I had the right. I said I'm curious. And I think you should be, too."

"What does that mean?"

"It just means if you're thinking of settling down and playing house with this guy, you might want to find out what you're getting yourself into. That's all."

Spot ambled over, and Brody reached into his pocket for a doggie treat.

"What about you?" Cat asked, trying and failing to rein in her wayward tongue. "Do you ever want kids?"

"No." He didn't hesitate. And he didn't smile.

Something kicked hard in Cat's chest. "Why?"

"That's a good question to ask someone who *does* want them. 'Why?'"

"You don't like children?"

"I like them. Well, I don't *dislike* them. I just think people should be made to get some kind of license to have them. Prove they're fit parents."

"Yeah, yeah, I've heard all that before—especially from confirmed bachelors terrified of giving up their independence and their bad habits and their little black books."

Something in the way she said that last part brought Brody's head up. Cat cursed inwardly and grabbed a cookie.

The grin returned. "My fault for leaving it lying around. And it's maroon, not black."

Her face burned. "It's also not that little."

The damn thing was bulging with women's

names, addresses and phone numbers, as well as the occasional scribbled reminder: birthday, dress size, wine preference, favorite night spot. Plus a few telling notations: "Clingy." "Kinky." "A+++."

What did a woman have to do to earn an A+++?

What grade had he given *her*?

Brody arched his back and rotated his shoulders. "You know what I could use right now? A shoulder rub." At her wary look he added, "What? You office moms don't do shoulder rubs?"

She sighed. "Yes. We do shoulder rubs."

"Great." He beckoned to her. "I'm all stiff."

Cat circled the table and stood behind Brody. During the last three days, she'd done everything humanly possible to avoid touching him. Now she stared down at his short, dark hair and, resisting the urge to smooth the willful waves, placed her hands on his shoulders over his white T-shirt. His flesh felt hard and hot through the thin material. His subtle masculine scent rose to her nostrils, making her recall things she didn't want to recall. She began kneading the tight muscles at the base of his neck.

He said, "Wait a sec," sat forward to pull off the shirt and settled back in the chair.

Cat scowled, her hands hovering an inch above his bare skin. She'd been on the alert for three days, determined to nip any untoward behavior in the bud. Did this qualify? The truth was, a simple shoulder rub was indeed within her job description, but there was nothing simple about this particular assignment.

"Something wrong?" he asked, without turning.

Only everything. Cat lowered her hands and took up where she'd left off. His skin was smooth and sun bronzed, and he hadn't been lying about the stiff muscles. As she rotated the heels of her palms and pressed inward with her thumbs, Brody moaned and let his head drop forward. Cat found his appreciative response unexpectedly gratifying, and she deepened the massage, leaning into him, isolating and working the muscle groups.

She'd given shoulder rubs before, but she couldn't recall having had so much shoulder to work with. She devoted herself to each side in turn, molding the tight, sinewy flesh until she felt it relax. His little grunts and sighs of pleasure brought a gentle smile to her lips.

"You are *so* good at this," he groaned, and raised his head with what seemed an extraordinary effort. He reached up and laid his hand over hers, brought it to his lips for a light kiss. "Your turn," he said, rising.

"What?"

He pressed her into his vacated seat and moved behind her. "When's the last time you had a shoulder rub?"

"That's *my* job, remember?" she said, trying to push out of the seat, only to be unceremoniously shoved back down.

"To you it's a job—to me, a delightful diversion."

Then his big, powerful hands went to work, and her next objection was lost in a shuddering moan of pure hedonistic bliss so intense it was practically sexual. Cat tried to laugh off her embarrassing reaction, but his magic fingers never let up, and all she could do was whimper.

"How's that?" he asked.

Her reply was unintelligible. He chuckled, the sound deep and rich, rolling over and through her. Cat collapsed onto the table, her cheek pillowed on her folded arms, her muscles turning to pudding under his talented hands.

He said, "This would be even better on bare skin."

She responded with a snort that said *nice try*.

His hands stroked down her back and up her sides. The little shock of pleasure as his fingertips grazed the sides of her breasts made her breath catch. He repeated the caress, and she told herself she really ought to stop him, this was dangerous territory, but it just felt too damn good. *Soon*, she told herself. In a minute. Maybe two.

Ten minutes later he finished with a few light strokes, squatted next to her and tucked her breeze-ruffled hair behind her ear. His penetrating gaze was softened by the hint of a smile.

"Feel like playing hooky?" he murmured, as his broad palm slowly moved down her spine to the waistband of her shorts. His knuckles glided back up her side, over her ribs, and lingered at the sensitive outer edge of her breast, skimming back and forth. Even through her shirt and bra the teasing feather strokes stole her wits.

Play hooky. Code for doing again what they'd done the other night. Her body hummed, from the tips of her breasts to the secret place that pulsed with desire for him.

Brody scooted closer and tipped his head onto the table so they were eye-to-eye. Sunlight slanted under the umbrella, glinting in his dark beard stubble and turning his twilight eyes to the clear bottomless blue of a secluded lagoon. His expression was both tender and intense, and her heart slammed into her ribs as she struggled to remind herself why she mustn't play hooky with this man.

He touched his lips to hers. Lightly. And again.

"Remember the terrace?" he whispered.

She remembered. The two of them venturing naked onto the penthouse terrace in the hot night after hours of loving. Standing at the rail staring into velvet shadows on shadows that should have been the bejeweled, midnight city watching in all directions. Brody moving behind her, their bodies instinctively angling, flexing, joining with the practiced ease of longtime lovers. Rocking together in a languid rhythm that needed no words.

Two becoming one in the dark.

Cat sat up. "Don't do this, Brody." He started to speak, and she hushed him with a finger to his lips. "Let's just get through the next month."

After a moment he rose and backed away, folded his arms over his bare chest. "So tell me. Did Mr. Perfect ever make it to New York?"

She thought fast. "Yes. We've been seeing

each other. He'll be in town for...for a few weeks." Perhaps Brody would stop trying to get her back in bed if he thought she was actively involved with Greg.

His expression, so warm and intimate only moments before, was now flat, unreadable. "Does he know about us?"

"That's none of your—"

"Does he?"

"No."

"What's the matter? You don't think he'd appreciate our little 'comedy of errors'?"

Cat got to her feet. "Look. If I could, I'd go back and undo that horrendous mistake. I'd like to forget it ever happened, but you seem determined to make that as difficult as possible. If this is how the next four weeks are going to be, I'm out of here, Brody, I swear it."

He snatched up his T-shirt and pulled it over his head. "You can walk. Go ahead." He made a sweeping gesture inviting her to do so. "I'm not holding you against your will."

She closed her eyes briefly, struggling with her temper. "And if I do?"

"You know the answer to that."

If she walked, Nana got an earful.

"I'll lose my job," Cat said. "I can't afford that, especially not—" She stopped abruptly.

He quirked an eyebrow, inviting her to continue.

Especially not now, when I might have a child to provide for.

She said, "You know you have me backed

into a corner. You *could* do the decent thing and just let me go."

Spot joined them, and Brody knelt to rough-house with him. "But I'm not a decent person, remember? I'm the lowest form of life, a purveyor of lies and smarmy innuendo. A destroyer of lives."

Cat let her silence express agreement. Her opinion of his livelihood was no secret.

"Driving Serena Milton to suicide was my finest career move," he said, rubbing the big animal's head. "That book sold in the millions. Hell, I paid off the mortgage on this house. Bought a boat—a big one."

His callous words saddened her. She realized she'd been trying to give Brody the benefit of the doubt. Despite her disapproval of what he did for a living, up till now she'd assumed his worst crimes were simply indifference and greed. She hadn't wanted to think him capable of this cold calculation.

Cat knew she'd let her innermost hopes and fears cloud her judgment. In truth, she didn't want to think the *father of her child* capable of this cold calculation. She swallowed her bleak disappointment and let the anger bubble to the surface.

"A boat, huh?" she sneered. "Don't tell me. You named it the *Serena.*"

"It was tempting. But I settled for *The Tramp.*"

After a moment Cat said, "Enlighten me."

"Charlie Chaplin. I'm a big fan of his—of all the comic greats of the big and little screens. Fields, Marx, Mostel, Brooks, Ball, Burnett..."

"I should've guessed. I can't recall you targeting any of that crowd for character assassination."

Whereas the subject of his current exposé was getting it with both barrels. She'd been appalled when Brody had shown her his research notes and the draft of the first few chapters of *Nolan Branigan: Sins and Secrets*. The subtitle had been borrowed from Branigan's most renowned film, for which he'd received the Academy Award for Best Actor.

A squirrel darted up a red maple at the edge of the property, and Spot lumbered off in lukewarm pursuit. Still kneeling, Brody gave Cat one of his lopsided teasing smiles. "You're still angry about Nolan Branigan."

She grabbed the milk glasses from the table. "I still don't see why, just because someone's in the limelight, a movie star, that gives you the right to savage his reputation. For money."

She stalked toward the house, and he followed, laughing.

"You just can't stand it that your big Irish heartthrob has weaknesses like everyone else," he said.

Cat entered the kitchen through the screen door, letting it slam on Brody. "Which you don't hesitate to exploit for a buck, no matter how much damage you cause. If someone's a celebrity, his personal problems become fodder for hacks like you—" She bit her lip. "I didn't mean to say that."

He laughed again, slinging the cookie plate onto the counter. "After everything else you've said, you're apologizing for calling me a hack? That's so cute."

"I don't even believe half of what you're writing. Nolan Branigan is a good person, a dedicated family man."

"That 'family man' has been messing around with other women since his wedding day. And then there's the question of his—how to put this politely?—ambiguous sexuality."

"You have no *proof* of that!"

He shrugged. "Close enough."

"Why does the public need to know, even if it's true? It's between him and his wife."

"His long-suffering wife, who's come close to divorcing him twice over his infidelities."

Cat poked a finger at Brody's chest. "Which you only found out by prying into their personal lives. If you publish that book with all this stuff in it, it'll be *your* fault if they divorce—if their three kids become the casualties of a broken family." Cat's voice had turned shrill. To her horror, her eyes stung.

"There are worse things for kids than a broken family. Why are you getting so worked up over this? I'd have thought you were too old to have crushes on movie stars."

She turned from him and wiped her eyes with her fingertips, took a couple of deep breaths.

"Cat?" His voice held concern. She felt his hand on her shoulder. "What is it?"

"Nothing." The less this man knew about her personal demons, the better. "I'm just...a little tired."

After a moment he said, "Is it the kids? That business about the broken—"

"It's nothing!" She shook off his hand and escaped up the stairs.

CAT WAS CONSTRUCTING a shopping list for Brody when his phone rang in the computer room. He was in the basement sorting his laundry. The housekeeper who came twice a week was on vacation, and he'd done his best to convince Cat that washing his dirty socks was the sort of motherly service that would make him feel all warm and nurtured. Instead she'd patiently instructed her client in the intricacies of water temperature and permanent press settings. He was forty years old, she'd pointed out. Didn't he think it was high time he learned to fend for himself?

"No."

"You know what they say." She'd shoved the bottle of bleach at him. "Give me a fish and I'll eat for a day. *Teach* me to fish and I'll eat for a lifetime."

"So I take it you know how to fish."

"What? No." She'd stepped back as he enthusiastically splashed bleach into the machine.

"Now's as good a time as any to learn," he said. "We'll take out *The Tramp*—"

"You are going to stay down here until that entire mountain of laundry is washed, dried and folded."

"And if I don't?" A devilish light had come into his eyes. "What'll you do—spank me?"

He'd started to advance on her and she'd beat

another hasty retreat. Cat wondered if she was destined to spend the next month running from her client like a startled rabbit.

She finally located the ringing phone on the floor under the latest issue of *Mad* magazine, and grabbed it up.

"Brody Mikhailov's office," she said.

"Who's this?"

Cat glared at the phone. "May I ask who's calling, please?"

"Leon Lopez. Brody's agent." His voice was rough as steel wool. "Are you the office mom?"

"Yes, I am. Cat Seabright."

"You don't sound very friendly, Cat. I thought you gals were supposed to be all warm and fuzzy."

"I am." She swept a pile of papers from the wing chair and plopped down on it. "I'm very warm and fuzzy."

"You know this was my idea, right? An office mom for Brody's birthday present?"

"Yes, I know." Cat squeezed the phone as she imagined her fingers around Leon Lopez's throat. "So I have you to thank for this assignment."

His bark of laughter had her jerking the phone from her ear. Did he know about that night? Had Brody told him about her? She prayed not. The more people who knew, the greater the chance it would get back to Nana.

He said, "I knew he'd be a handful. You a looker?"

"What?"

"You know—are you a good-looking babe?"

"My face hasn't stopped any clocks lately."

"Then I'm not even gonna ask if he's keeping his hands to himself. Just smack him around if he gets too frisky."

Good. He didn't know.

"Thank you, Mr. Lopez. I'll keep that in mind."

"Call me Leon. Listen, kiddo, I'm counting on you to give me my money's worth. I could've bought that boy a set of luggage for his birthday. Season tickets to the Giants. Hell, I could've hired him a high-class hooker!"

Cat sagged in the chair, rubbing her temple.

"But I've known Brody for almost twenty years," Leon said. "I know what he really needs. Even if he doesn't."

"TLC," she murmured, recalling the conversation in Nana's office. *How did Leon put it? A little TLC might have a humanizing effect on me.*

"Bingo!" Leon cried. "Tender loving care. Which, since he's never had any, he won't know what to do with, but don't let that stop you."

Before Cat could ask what he meant by that, he said, "Oh! The reason I called. Tell Brody I'm flying out to L.A. tomorrow, gonna do lunch with Schneider and Serrano." He singsonged, "Tell him it's look-ing go-od."

"Serrano? Pia Serrano?" Cat asked, referring to the 1980s sitcom actress who now hosted one of those smarmy daytime talk shows.

"Yeah, she's the talent, though I personally think Schneider should've held out for someone hotter."

"Wait. Brody's involved in TV?"

"He didn't tell you? With any luck, our boy'll be head writer for a new prime-time network newsmagazine that's in the works. They're calling it *Banner Headline*. Gonna highlight a different celeb each week—dead celebs mostly, to cut down on slander suits. Kind of like those books he writes, but in one-hour doses for a viewership in the millions. *Biography* meets the *National Enquirer*."

Just when she thought Brody couldn't go any lower, he sheds his skin and slithers under the doors of a new batch of bedrooms—and mausoleums. Dead celebs mostly, huh? She shuddered, thinking of Serena Milton.

Leon continued, "He's got stiff competition for the job, but let's face it. Nobody slings the mud like Brody. He's the King of Sling. Like I said, it's look-ing go-od."

5

"IT'S LOOK-ING GO-OD," Brody warbled, as he closed the oven door on the bubbling lasagna. "Smelling good, too."

"Been talking to Leon, have you?" Cat pulled aside the kitchen curtain and peered out at the rain battering the backyard.

"I'm always talking to Leon. Why?"

Instead of answering, she said, "You were wrong. The rain's not letting up—it's getting worse. I really think I'm going to have to knock off early, Brody. I have a long drive home."

She was supposed to stay until eight. It was now five-thirty. "But I'm actually *cooking*, Cat. I'm making history here! No part of this meal had anything to do with the telephone or take-out menus. You *have* to stay."

During the two weeks that she'd been Brody's office mom, Cat had made him start laying in fresh food, the kind that required some degree of preparation and was presumably better for him than the Colonel's extra crispy and microwave burritos. She'd watched him cook for Spot often enough; he couldn't claim he didn't know how.

On several occasions Cat had scribbled shopping lists and dragged him to the grocery store—a real supermarket, not the pricey convenience store he usually patronized—where he'd learned how to grope mangoes and eyeball expiration dates. She seemed determined to turn him into a responsible, self-sufficient adult.

He slit a loaf of Italian bread and started spreading garlic butter on it. "Besides, if you leave now, you'll hit rush hour."

She dropped the curtain and turned to him. "Going *toward* the city?"

"Well, once you're past the city, it'll be bumper to bumper heading north. You know that. You're better off waiting. Maybe the rain'll let up."

"Mmm...maybe."

"*Or* you could take me up on my standing offer of the guest room. It wouldn't take me five minutes to clear all that stuff off the bed and throw some sheets on it."

Her expression didn't change, but she crossed her arms over her chest. He doubted she was aware of the eloquence of her body language.

"Scout's honor." He held up a butter-smeared hand. "I'll be good. No tiptoeing into your room in the middle of the night."

She looked away. "That's all right. I'd rather be home. But thanks anyway."

He wrapped the bread in foil and shoved it in the oven. "Is it Mr. Perfect? Afraid he'll object if you spend the—"

"No. I mean, maybe. He...he wouldn't like it."

Brody placed a ripe tomato on the wooden

cutting board and split it with a sharp kitchen knife. "Why would he have to know?"

She hugged herself tighter. "I couldn't lie to Greg. I believe in honesty."

Brody kept his eyes on the tomato he was slicing. *Whack. Whack.* "Like you were honest with him about you and me?"

She didn't answer, and he slashed the tomato with increasing zeal. *Whack! Whack! Whack!* Hadn't she told him she wanted to forget it ever happened—their "horrendous mistake"? *Whack!*

A raw curse erupted as blood oozed from his finger.

"Let me see it." Cat was by his side immediately, grabbing for his hand.

"It's nothing," he said, pulling away.

She fought him for possession of the wounded digit. "Looks deep. You may need stitches."

"No!"

"Oh, come on, it's not the end of the—"

"*No!* No stitches."

She sighed. "All right. Let's get the bleeding stopped and I'll take a closer look. Sit down."

Cat shoved him into a chair, grabbed a clean paper napkin, folded it and pressed it to the finger, holding his arm vertical. She was a paragon of efficiency. Normally he had no patience with efficient people, but something about her brisk, take-charge attitude made him feel...well, nurtured.

After a couple of minutes she eased the bloody napkin away and peered at the injury, a half-inch gash. "Okay, the bleeding's mostly stopped. I think we can get away with a butterfly."

"What's that?"

"It's like stitches, only worse."

"Ha ha ha," he heard himself say, chagrined at having picked up his office mom's most annoying expression.

"Hold this," she said, turning the napkin and pressing it back on the wound. Before leaving the kitchen, she checked the lasagna and bread, and turned off the oven. She was back shortly with a few first aid supplies and a pair of scissors, with which she cut a small piece of adhesive tape and notched it on both sides. She held it up for him to see. "Butterfly."

"Bow tie."

"What?"

"It looks more like a bow tie than a—"

"Shut up and sit still."

She cleaned his finger with peroxide and let it dry. He watched in fascination as she carefully placed the bow tie across the cut, holding the skin closed.

"Isn't that clever," he said.

"I didn't make this up. They sell butterfly bandages ready-made, but you didn't have any."

"How do you know how to do this?"

She shrugged. "I guess I just picked it up."

She unwrapped a bandage and squirted a little antibiotic cream on it, then applied it to the wound. Brody watched her slim fingers gently smooth down the plastic strip. Her nails were short, adorned only with a little clear polish. She wore a narrow band of braided silver on her pinky.

Her hand lingered on his and he looked up at her face, inches away. Her pale azure eyes seemed to hold a question. For him? For herself? Time lengthened, quivered, stretched tight as a drum. Rain that sounded like gravel drilled the window glass. Cat glanced down at their joined hands and stepped back.

"I'll finish the salad," she said.

"Cat—"

"Do you want wine with dinner?" Her tone was nonchalant, in contrast to her stilted movements as she reached into the refrigerator for lettuce.

Brody almost said, *Can we talk about this? This thing simmering between us? It's not going to go away.* Then he remembered Mr. Perfect and was forced to acknowledge that this thing between them might be more one-sided than he wanted to admit. Maybe Cat and Greg had a hot date lined up for tonight. That would explain her eagerness to get home.

He realized he didn't want to know. His mind began to form a picture of Cat and her lover together in bed, doing the things Brody had done with her that night.

"Well?" she said. "Wine?"

"Vodka. I'll get it." He got up and retrieved the bottle from the freezer, and poured a liberal dose into the first thing that came to hand, a large coffee mug embellished with a reproduction of Edward Hopper's moody painting *Nighthawks*. He barely felt the first long swallow. Cat was pretending not to notice as she dried the lettuce in the spinner and emptied it into a handmade ceramic salad bowl.

Spot whined at the back door. Brody let him in and hustled out of range as he shook rainwater off his fur. The dog took an interest in his master's neatly bandaged finger, which Brody held away from him. "Thanks anyway, boy, but that's my office mom's job, to kiss my boo-boo all better." To Cat he said, "Isn't that what moms do?"

"Is that what your mom did?" She rinsed a green pepper and started to cut it, but stopped to look at him when he failed to answer.

The only thing more pathetic than a drunk lusting after an unavailable woman was a motherless drunk lusting after an unavailable woman. Brody ignored the question and set about pouring Cat a generous glass of burgundy, resolved not to get hammered alone.

"I don't want that much," she said, eyeing the overfull wineglass. "I have to drive tonight."

"So don't finish it." He set the bottle on the table.

Cat did indeed finish her wine during dinner, absently sipping it while they decimated the lasagna and debated which of Mel Brooks's movies was the most sidesplitting. Brody surreptitiously topped off her glass a couple of times.

Finally she sat back, replete and glassy-eyed. "You said it would stop." She yawned, gesturing languidly at the rain-lashed window.

"I said maybe." He lifted the wine bottle.

She waved away his attempt to refill her glass and came sluggishly to her feet.

"Leave the dishes," he said, rising and steering her out of the kitchen toward the living room. He grabbed his cigarettes off the counter on the way. "You want coffee?"

"No." She checked her watch. "Damn, Brody, you did that on purpose."

"What?" He settled them on the powder blue camelback sofa and switched on the table lamp, casting the room in a warm glow.

"You got me tipsy," she said. "You knew I had to drive."

"Hey, don't blame me for what you imbibe. You want a brandy?"

"*No,* I don't want a brandy!" She slumped against the sofa, her head thrown back.

Brody himself was somewhere on the far side of tipsy, contentedly so. He slid a cigarette from the pack, and Cat groaned.

"Do you have to?"

Normally he'd have said something like, *No, but I'm going to anyway.* Instead he held the cigarette poised at his lips for a moment, then tapped it back into the pack.

"Thanks," she said, and he could tell he'd surprised her. He'd surprised them both.

Brody draped an arm on the sofa back behind her. Strands of silky copper-colored hair teased the sensitive inside of his elbow, below the sleeve of his navy blue T-shirt. "Now you have to do a favor for me."

Her smirk spoke volumes. "And what might that be?"

His muzzy mind hadn't gotten that far. "Uh…you have to play strip poker with me."

"Oh yeah, that's real nurturing."

"Okay, how about…you give me a nice soothing bubble bath. Wash my back."

"I'm not that drunk, Brody."

"So I guess naked mayonnaise wrestling is out of the question."

"I never said that. Regular or low-fat?"

"I only have regular."

She threw up her hands in mock disappointment. He slipped his fingers down to her satiny shoulder, bared by her sleeveless apricot-colored top.

"Have I ever told you I have a thing for mayonnaise?" he asked.

She looked at his hand on her shoulder, then at his face. "Is that so?"

"Just the thought of you covered in all that slippery, shiny—"

"Slimy, don't forget slimy."

He stroked her upper arm, taking care not to scrape her with the bandage. "Slathered in mayo from head to toe. And with only one way to get it off."

"Can I assume this one way has nothing to do with soap and water?"

He stared into her crystal blue eyes, their gaze slightly unfocused. He said, "Only the human tongue can do a really thorough job."

"Gee, I never saw that one coming."

"A task like that takes heroic patience and attention to detail. It's not a job for your average tongue."

Cat looked away. But not before her eyes flicked to his mouth.

"It takes flexibility," he continued. "Stamina. All those nooks and crannies. I'm a nook man myself, but crannies have their charm."

He leaned in close, drawing her scent into his lungs, that faint woodsy-floral fragrance that had driven him half mad that first night, when he'd been unable to see her, when he'd had to rely on his other, underused senses.

He said, "It'd take a long time to lick it all off. Where would be the best place to start, do you think?" He turned her face and made her look at him. Her pupils were dilated, her cheeks rosier than before. "You think about where and I'll see if I can guess."

She tried to avert her face, but he refused to let her. He smiled. "That would've been my choice, too."

"You fraud. You don't know what I'm thinking."

"Betcha I do."

"Betcha you don't."

"Here?" He slid his fingers under her knee, exposed by her black denim shorts, and lightly stroked the soft skin there.

She made a funny little sound and said in a choked voice, "No."

"Really. How about here?" He traced a path between her breasts as she tried to flatten herself against the sofa.

"Uh-uh," she said.

"I know." His fingers glided along the smooth inside of her thigh and under the hem of her shorts. She grabbed his wrist and clamped her legs together, effectively trapping his hand there, though he doubted that was her intention.

"That's it, isn't it?" he asked. "That's the place."

Her voice was breathless. "It took you three guesses."

His fingertips were at the very top of her thigh. He lightly caressed the baby-soft skin. "I remember how sensitive you are here."

"That's enough." She tried in vain to move his hand.

"I believe I may have scratched you here with my whiskers—" he rubbed his bristly cheek "—ungroomed barbarian that I am. Did I hurt you?"

"No. Yes. A little. But it was okay."

"It was okay? You liked it?"

"I didn't say that." She arched a bit as his fingers inched north, to the elastic leg opening of her panties. "Maybe. A little."

If he hadn't plied her with demon alcohol, he'd never have made it this far, he knew. Hell, he'd never have made it past her shoulder. If she were stone-cold sober, there'd now be fresh skid marks on his driveway.

"Where else did I scratch you?" he asked.

No answer.

"Here?" He brushed his free hand over her breasts, and the stiff nipples that pushed against her shirt. She made a strangled sound. This game was getting him hard, fueling his impatience. "Hmm?"

"Yes," she whispered.

"I wish I could've seen that," he said, imagining her sprawled beneath him, her tender skin glowing pink in the most interesting places, him kissing it all better. "All that incredible sex we had, and I've never seen you naked."

Cat's breasts rose and fell in an agitated rhythm. Her grip on his wrist had eased, and her shorts were loose enough to let him explore a bit. Her eyes drifted shut as his fingertips crept along the edge of her panties. Her mouth was slightly open, and he didn't even try to resist it.

She jumped a little when Brody's lips covered hers. He inhaled her wine-sweet breath and her ragged moan as he touched her through her silky panties. His fingertips traced the shape of her, lingered at the womanly cleft, testing the slippery dampness there.

He smiled as a delicious whimper escaped her. She turned toward him, her legs opening, her hands clutching. Brody's erection was savage and insistent, a beast of prey, howling for the succulent quarry so near at hand. But he knew what kind of man took advantage of an inebriated woman, and he'd always prided himself on never having crossed that line.

He thought about sending Cat home in her current state of arousal, all ripe and ready for Mr. Perfect.

The hell with it; he'd find something else to pride himself on. He deepened the kiss and the intimate caress. Cat shuddered in his arms, moving against him. He started yanking her shirt out of the waistband of her shorts.

A sharp yip broke through the haze of blind thumping need.

"Go away, Spot."

The big animal had parked himself at their feet, tail swinging, ready to join in this fun new game. Dazed and rumpled, Cat blinked at him.

"Go *away*, Spot!" Brody jabbed his finger toward the kitchen. "Go!"

Spot gave two more gleeful barks and placed his forepaws on Cat's lap. She straightened and seemed to notice for the first time that her shirt was untucked. Brody cursed inwardly. *It's the canned stuff for you from now on,* he silently promised the aging mutt. *The bargain brand.*

"I—I think the rain is letting up." She squinted, trying to see through the front windows and the enclosed porch. "Sounds like it, anyway." Pushing Spot off her, she stood and righted her clothing.

Brody came to his feet, glaring at man's best friend until the animal slunk out of the room. "I can't let you drive like this. You've been drinking."

She skewered him with a sardonic look. "Something tells me I'm safer on the roads."

"Cat...look, stay here. I promise I won't try anything."

"Don't worry about me," she said, grabbing her purse from the chair where she'd left it and retrieving her car keys. "This has been a very sobering experience."

"Take a cab. I'll pay for it." He sighed in exasperation as she ignored him and stepped outside into the evening drizzle. Guilt nagged him.

In truth, she hadn't drunk that much, less than two glasses, but he still didn't want her driving. It was his fault. If he hadn't pushed his luck, she wouldn't be bolting now.

"Call me when you get home," he said from the front doorway, though he knew she wouldn't. "Let me know you got there okay."

He watched her slam the door of her white sedan. She left skid marks on his driveway.

6

"SO HE COOKS DINNER for you." Brigit hurled herself into the empty barber chair next to the one Cat occupied and spun it in a circle. "That's very romantic."

"You don't know this guy," Cat said, as Ren tipped her head forward. "There's nothing romantic about Brody. He's just after sex."

"You say that like it's a bad thing," Ren said, twisting the top layers of Cat's wet hair and securing them with clips. "What's wrong with a romp?"

"She's had the romp," Brigit informed him. "Now she doesn't want anything to do with him."

"Ahh!" Ren's scissors felt cold on Cat's nape as he snipped off the usual half inch. "Poor guy didn't measure up, huh?"

"He measured up *too* well!" Brigit said.

"Brigit!" Cat jerked her head around, earning a growl of disapproval from Ren, who firmly repositioned her. "The whole world doesn't need to know my business."

"And she's had to work side by side with him every day for a month," Brigit said. From the corner of her eye Cat watched her friend lift a hand mirror from the workstation and wipe lipstick off her teeth.

"But at least today's my last day with Brody," Cat said, as Ren tilted her head up and met her eyes in the wall-to-wall salon mirror. The hairdresser was tan and fit, with a salt-and-pepper buzz cut and appealingly craggy features. Cat had been going to him for years.

"So you just don't like this guy," he said.

She opened her mouth to disagree, and snapped it shut. She *didn't* like Brody Mikhailov. There was just so much not to like about him, from his self-absorbed life-style to what he did for a living. And to top it all off, Leon had recently divulged that Brody was close to being offered the head-writer job for that horrible new TV show, *Banner Headline*. It was now a close race between Brody and Mildred Maxwell, doyenne of the gossip columns.

"He's got this old dog," Cat heard herself say, wondering where that had come from. "A real creaker. You should see how Brody takes care of him. I mean, he coddles him. Cooks *meals* for him."

"Oh yeah," Brigit said, squirting a ball of hair mousse onto her palm to play with. "Sounds like one well-adjusted guy."

Cat started to turn toward her, only to have her head wrenched back in place. "There's nothing wrong with wanting to be good to your pet when he gets old," she declared. "Spot's been with Brody forever. It's…well, it's sweet, really. He cares for him as if he were a baby."

Brigit said, "Speaking of babies…"

Cat tried to glower at her sideways. Ren paused in his snipping. "What's this?" he asked. "Are you—"

"No! I'm not pregnant!"

"Who's pregnant?" Marina, Ren's wife, called through the packed salon, from her post at the reception desk.

"Cat," he answered. "Only she says she's not."

"How do you know?" Brigit asked Cat. "You haven't even done the test."

"I know, okay? I'm not pregnant."

The manicurist looked up from the acrylic nail she was filing. "Who's pregnant?"

Ren said, "How many periods have you missed?"

Cat groaned as Brigit answered for her. "One. She was due three weeks ago."

"*Almost* three weeks," Cat said. "Nineteen days."

"Are you regular?" He crossed in front of her to pull side strands forward and compare length.

"Yes. No! I've been known to be late."

"*Three weeks* late?" Brigit asked.

"Has she missed her period?" Marina hollered.

"One," her husband answered. "Three weeks ago."

"Nineteen days!" Cat said.

"Who missed a period?" the shampoo girl yelled.

"That one." Her customer pointed out Cat. "Pay attention."

"Oh God," Cat whimpered.

"When are you going to get around to doing the test?" Ren asked, picking up the blow dryer.

"I'm not pregnant!"

A woman across the room put down her magazine and raised the hood of her dryer, displaying a rubber highlighting helmet covered with pasty white bleach and a thin shower cap. "Who's pregnant?"

"You know what they call this," Brigit said, as she pawed through a drawer full of pins, combs and tip money. "They call this denial."

"Shut up, Brigit."

"She wants a baby, but she doesn't want to have anything to do with the guy. And it's way too late to not have anything to do with this guy. Plus she's got the hots for him something fierce."

Ren turned on the blessedly loud blow dryer, then turned it off to ask, "Are your breasts tender?"

"That is none of your business!"

"Marina's breasts were real tender with all three of our kids. Even before she missed her first—"

"Would you just dry my hair?"

Brigit had to shout to be heard over the whine of the dryer. *"There's nothing to those drugstore tests. You just pee on a stick!"*

"You really should do that," Ren hollered. "Then you'd know for sure."

A middle-aged woman with a stiffly lacquered helmet of violet hair patted Cat's shoulder on her way out of the salon. "Congratulations, dear."

"Would you people get a life?" Cat shrieked. "I am *not pregnant!*"

CAT RANG THE BELL three times before Brody finally jerked the door open. The cordless phone was at his ear and he wore a murderous scowl.

"That job was supposed to be *mine!*" He stalked back into the house without acknowledging her. "Is Schneider on *drugs?* How much of a say did Serrano have in this, that's what I want to know. She's always been buddy-buddy with Maxwell."

Mildred Maxwell. The *Banner Headline* job. Cat set her purse on a chair. He must be talking to Leon.

Brody threw up his hand. "That old tattletale hasn't had an original thought since 1961. She's been coasting for decades. Her column's a *joke!*"

Cat followed at a cautious distance as he stomped into the dining room, where the table was laden with cartons containing hundreds of author's copies of his many books. Angry color flooded his face; veins stood out in his neck.

"That job was supposed to be *mine*, Leon! Don't tell me to calm down, damn it! When am I going to get another chance like this?" Brody paused, then added, "Don't bother."

He turned off the phone and flung it onto the sideboard; it bounced off a massive ashtray carved from a petrified log and crashed to the floor. Spot emerged from under the table and hied himself off to the kitchen. Brody charged after him and snatched up his cigarettes as the dog slipped back into the dining room.

Cat stood silently in the kitchen doorway. She'd never seen Brody like this. For the first time, she realized just how much that head-writer job had meant to him. His movements stiff and mechanical, he dragged deeply on his cigarette, making an obvious effort to deal with his anger and disappointment.

Finally she said, "I'm sorry, Brody," and surprised herself by meaning it.

Her words seemed to jog him out of his own dark thoughts. "Don't," he said, spearing her with a caustic glare she'd never seen before. "The last thing I need is you spouting bogus platitudes at me." He threw open the freezer door and pulled out the bottle of vodka.

Cat looked at her feet. "I can't blame you for doubting my sincerity, after everything I've said about...your career and all. But I mean it, Brody. I wish this had worked out for you. I know how much you wanted it."

Brody stared at her for long moments, expressionless. He looked away and took another drag of his cigarette. At last he acknowledged her statement with a terse nod.

When he grabbed a juice glass and uncapped the bottle, she took a deep breath and stepped into the kitchen. "Listen, why don't we get out of here. We could both use a change of scenery." Somehow she couldn't stomach the prospect of Brody spending their last few hours together in a haze of boozy self-pity.

He was quiet so long she suspected he hadn't

heard her. Finally he stubbed out his cigarette and listlessly recapped the bottle. "Where do you want to go?"

"DON'T YOU THINK you're carrying this mom thing a little too far?" Brody asked as Cat buckled the worn leather safety belt around his waist and hoisted herself onto the painted horse next to his.

"When was the last time you were at an amusement park?" she responded, as the carousel began moving to the accompaniment of old-fashioned calliope music.

"If this is supposed to make me forget my troubles, I have a better suggestion."

His leer left little question as to the nature of that suggestion, but there was no real heat behind it. Cat knew a diversionary tactic when she saw one, and it occurred to her that after working with Brody for a month, she knew nothing of his upbringing. He'd managed to dance around the topic every time it came up.

Then again, hadn't she done the same thing herself? With good reason, of course—no entanglements and all that—but she had to admit she'd been no more forthcoming than he.

Their colorful mounts rose and dipped in perfect counterpoint as the circular wooden deck revolved. At the center of the structure were ancient beveled mirrors. Cat stared at them, at the wavering, kaleidoscopic images rushing past, trying to catch her own reflection. Every time she thought she had it, it winked out of sight.

That had been a mistake, looking at those mirrors. She closed her eyes for a moment, willing away the brief wave of disorientation. That was all it was, she assured herself. It wasn't nausea. And anyway, this wasn't the morning, so it couldn't possibly be—

Stop that! she commanded herself. *You're not!*

Grasping for conversation, she said, "There aren't too many of these old carousels left. This one's about eighty-five years old."

"Seriously?"

She nodded. "It was bought secondhand sixty years ago when this place opened. These horses are hand carved. Oh! Grab the ring!"

"What?" He looked around anxiously, his fingers tightening on the brass pole.

My God, Cat thought, *he's never done this before.* The revelation squeezed her heart.

Brody was on the outside horse. She pointed to the slim metal arm, fast approaching, that jutted toward the carousel. "Grab a ring when you pass that. If you're lucky, you'll get the brass one."

She watched comprehension dawn—the proverbial "brass ring"!—followed by a look of determination so fierce she didn't know whether to laugh, or to cry for the lost boy who she suspected had missed out on more than carousel rides and boo-boo kisses.

As Brody passed the metal arm, he raised himself off the painted saddle and stretched far out to snatch a ring from the business end of the contraption. He lunged for it, gripping the pole for balance, as the old leather stirrups creaked under his weight and all kinds of interesting muscle groups bunched and flexed.

He showed Cat the steel ring he'd snagged. "What happens if I get the brass?"

"You turn it in for a free ride."

"They don't let you keep it?"

"Nope."

He was already on the lookout for the metal arm as it came around again. "All right, I've got a few more tries."

After several more unsuccessful attempts, the calliope music began to slow, along with the horses. As the metal arm came within reach, Brody leaned out and made one last grab.

"Hah! Will you look at that!" He twirled the gleaming brass ring around his finger.

Cat laughed, absurdly happy for him, pleased beyond measure to see his smile return, on today of all days. As he passed the ring dispenser, Brody tossed the steel rings he'd collected into the plastic bucket hanging from it. She was about to remind him that he had a free ride coming, until she saw him slip something into his jeans pocket as he dismounted.

One large building housed the carousel and snack bar. Outside were kiddie rides and a miniature golf course. This was a small neighborhood amusement park, swarming with mothers and their young children on a Wednesday afternoon in August.

Cat and Brody sauntered around the inside perimeter of the building, where assorted diversions encircled the carousel. Along one wall was a bank of video games as well as a handful of old-fashioned pinball machines. Brody's steps slowed as he started rhapsodizing about his college days as the Pinball Wizard. Cat said she wasn't surprised, and kept him moving with a firm grip on his elbow.

They passed a glass-enclosed booth in which a beturbaned plaster fortune teller, Madame Zena, held playing cards fanned in her stiff fingers. They stopped to watch a couple of preadolescent girls feed her a coin. The metallic grating of an antiquated motor accompanied Madame Zena's unbecoming jerks and twitches, this impressive display culminating in the spewing of a fortune card from a slot.

One of the girls grabbed the card and read it, her lips moving silently. "Oh-my-God!" she squealed, with a flash of braces. She shared the card with her friend, and the two girls collapsed in giggles.

Cat and Brody turned a corner and passed a family playing Skee-Ball, rolling balls up an incline, aiming for the highest-scoring circular trough.

"I don't remember this place being so… retro," Cat said.

"You came here as a kid?"

She nodded. "My mom used to take me here all the time. Come on—I'll buy you an ice-cream cone."

A few minutes later, soft-serve vanilla cones in hand, they strolled outside, watching the horde of children on the Ferris wheel, in the tame little roller coaster, in the miniature wooden boats and cars and airplanes. The sun shone bright and hot in a cloudless sky.

They stopped and leaned against a chain-link fence, watching a little girl furiously spin the wheel of a handcar rolling along a looping track. She plowed into the car in front of her, occupied by a lethargic boy twice her size, and with scarlet-faced tenacity propelled them both to the end of the course.

The ice cream tasted like summer, like childhood, when her most pressing concern had been licking it all up before it melted down her hand. Cat glanced at Brody, who was quietly observing the throngs of boisterous youngsters. He didn't share her sticky-sweet nostalgia, she knew. Somehow, she just knew.

"It's very important to you, isn't it?" she said, and he looked at her. "Making your mark. Achieving recognition."

He took his time answering.

She nodded toward his drippy, droopy ice cream. "That's going to be all over your hand in about another second."

He heeded her warning, and in moments he'd finished off the whole thing, cone and all.

"Well?" she asked.

"I'm not sure what you want to hear. Isn't success important to everyone?"

"To varying degrees—and for varying reasons."

"Don't you want to be a success?" he asked. "Achieve recognition?"

"As an office mom?" She smiled.

"Perhaps as a dry run for the real thing."

Cat's smile faded.

"I said it before." With his thumb he wiped ice cream off the corner of her mouth. "You're very good at it."

She didn't like how this conversation was getting turned around. "You mean you wouldn't demand that I get a license to reproduce?" she asked, recalling their conversation at his picnic table.

Do you ever want kids? she'd asked him.

No. He'd felt that people should have to prove they'd be fit parents.

Did Brody consider himself unfit for parenthood?

"It seems to come naturally to you," he said. "I think you have a strong maternal streak."

Cat looked down, fixed her watery gaze on her cone. Her chin quivered.

"Cat...what did I say?"

His tender bewilderment was her undoing. A tear rolled down her cheek and she swiped at it. "Oh God..." She dreaded becoming a bawling spectacle for the raucous young families swarming around them.

Brody wrestled the remains of her cone out of her hand and tossed it in a nearby trash basket. His arm came around her and he guided her to an isolated corner of the fence bordering the miniature golf course. He kept her back to the crowd milling around the roller coaster, which rumbled along its diminutive track, every mild dip punctuated by earsplitting shrieks.

"I'm sorry." Cat took a deep, shuddering breath and ransacked her purse for a tissue. "I just seem to be...a little emotional lately. It's stupid. I'm sorry."

He threaded his fingers through the hair at her temple, a half smile on his face. "Maybe it's just, you know, that time of the month? Women sometimes get a little weepy...."

The possibility cheered her. "I think I may be a bit, uh, premenstrual." She blew her nose.

"We passed a little Irish pub down the road. Let me buy you a beer."

"No. No, thanks."

"Come on, a drink is just the thing for what ails you. At least, that's what I've been told."

"I couldn't, I..." She knew why she couldn't, why she wouldn't, even as a stubborn part of her chanted, *I'm not, I'm not, I'm not....* "Beer makes me sleepy," she said.

"So?"

"So then I'll be sleepy *and* weepy."

"Sleepy and Weepy. Aren't they related to the Seven Dwarves?"

"The Seven *PMS* Dwarves: Sleepy, Weepy, uh...Crampy, Groggy..."

"Cranky, Antsy..."

"And Bloated."

Brody leaned back against the fence and gave Cat an appreciative once-over. "I don't see any bloat. Must be a misdiagnosis."

Lord, I hope not. "You never answered my question. You're very good at that, by the way. Evading direct questions."

"Thank you."

"I asked you about recognition, its importance to you."

"What's important to me right now is getting you onto my boat." He glanced at the position of the sun, high in the western sky. "It's still early—"

"Oh no, you don't," she said, chuckling, even as the mere mention of a boat brought on another surge of nausea—no, not nausea, *disorientation*, she reminded herself. "Stick to the subject."

He studied her for long moments. "Why do you want to know this?"

Why indeed? Whatever happened to no entanglements? "I'm just curious about what drives you, what would drive anyone to write fifty-some-odd books—"

"Fifty-seven."

"Fifty-seven books in nineteen years, and now this TV thing—" She bit her tongue.

Brody gave her a wry smile. "I'm not going to slit my wrists over 'this TV thing,' Cat. You can mention it."

She leaned next to him against the fence. "I've seen the scrapbooks you keep, all the reviews, articles about you and your career. Two decades worth." She looked at him. "They're not very flattering, Brody. Some of them are downright virulent." Not about his writing ability, which was universally praised, but about the content of his work.

"You know what they say. Any publicity is good publicity."

"What, they can say anything they like as long as they spell your name right?"

He spread his arms, his smile impish. "Hey, at

least they're not ignoring me. You think it's easy generating that level of virulence?"

She stared at him as the pieces began falling into place. "I'll bet you were a real hell-raiser when you were a kid."

"How'd you guess?"

"You must've kept your parents hopping."

"My office mom, now, she has the patience of a saint. Though she refuses to tuck me in at night. Why do you suppose that is?"

More evasions. He'd honed the skill to a fine art.

She asked, "How do they feel about what you do for a living?"

"Who?"

"Your parents."

His expression settled into a kind of weary defeat. Now he was going to tell her to mind her own business, since she clearly couldn't take a hint.

"Are they gone?" she asked quietly. "Dead?"

He sighed, gazing at the little roller coaster discharging its passengers. "One of them is, that I know of."

The flatness of his tone chilled her.

"My mother," he said. "She died twelve years ago of cirrhosis."

"I'm sorry."

"Don't be. I didn't really know her."

Cat waited.

Brody watched as children climbed into the roller coaster. An overweight youth in a Mets cap collected tickets and lowered the metal guard bar in each car, before pulling the lever to start the motor.

Brody glanced at Cat, briefly. "My mother was a drunk. They took me away from her when I was a toddler." He patted his pockets, obviously looking for the cigarettes he'd left in the car. "She'd neglected me, didn't much mind giving me up. That's what I was told."

"Your father?"

"No one knows who he was," Brody said. "Probably not even my mother."

"Who raised you?"

"A whole bunch of foster families."

Cat frowned. "Why a whole bunch?"

"No one wanted to keep me. Even at three and a half, when I entered the system, I was a handful."

No wonder, if he'd suffered enough under his mother to be taken from her. Cat thought of Brody as a helpless little boy, acting out in a futile bid for love and attention, being shuttled from one set of indifferent strangers to another—and felt like weeping again.

"So you never saw your mother after that?" she asked.

He folded his arms, staring at the roller coaster. "She basically washed her hands of me when she lost custody. But I looked her up when I was seventeen, about to graduate from high school. I thought maybe she'd want to go to my graduation." With a bitter chuckle he added, "I had this stupid sentimental notion of my mom sitting out there, proud as hell, watching her little boy receive his diploma."

Cat's throat constricted. "It didn't work out?"

Brody sighed. "I don't know what I expected. No, that's not true. I'd built up this whole big fantasy in my mind. That she'd changed, cleaned up her act. That she really did want me, wanted us to be a family."

Cat started to speak, and stopped. The only things she could think to say would sound too much like pity.

"When I met her again, after all those years, she was...well, she was a pathetic excuse for a human being, much less a mother." He was silent a few moments before adding, "Years later, when I learned she'd died, I paid for the funeral. But I didn't go."

Minutes passed. Brody still stared at the roller coaster, but Cat didn't think he was seeing it. "I've never told anyone about her," he said quietly.

"I'm glad you told me."

He looked at her then, and she held out her hand. Slowly he unfolded his arms and twined his fingers with hers. She answered his sad little smile with one of her own.

"You didn't go to your graduation, did you?" she asked.

He shook his head. "What would have been the point? With no one there to watch?"

Cat dragged in a deep breath, fighting the ache in her heart. She squeezed his hand.

He said, "Sometimes I wonder if he's still alive."

"Who? Your father?"

He nodded. "And if he's read my books and

what he'd think of me if I'd ended up with *Banner Headline*."

Brody was still acting out, she realized, with his outrageous career choices, his abrasive, in-your-face public persona in the form of Jake Beckett. He was seeking validation, or at least attention—a poor substitute for the unconditional love that should have been his as a child.

"Brody, have you ever considered writing…something different?"

She wished she could wipe that crooked grin off his face.

"You know, a departure from your usual, um, biographies," Cat said. "I mean, you have to be tired of writing the same old…" She hesitated.

"Oh, please tell me my Little Orphan Brody story hasn't taken the razor edge off your talons. It has," he groaned. "You're going to get all tactful on me now."

"Tired of writing the same old sensationalist trash!" she finished. "Okay? Are you happy now?"

"Ecstatic. All the support and encouragement I've come to expect from my office mom. And what might this 'something different' be that you think I should write? Cookbooks? Children's stories?"

"The comic greats!" she cried, ignoring his sarcasm. "A history of the funniest of the funny, from the movies and TV. You love those guys, Brody!"

"You're talking about—what? A coffee-table book." Judging from his grimace, she might have been suggesting he take up a career in medical waste management.

"Now, hear me out!" she demanded. "This would be a way to expand your readership, establish yourself as a serious biographer."

"I don't write puff."

"I'm not talking puff. You can give a thorough and honest—and respectful—accounting of a celebrity's life without whitewashing it. I know you've compiled information over the years about Chaplin and Fields and all those guys. I've seen your files, the clippings and notes."

"That's called an interest, a hobby. Not research. I've spent nineteen years building a reputation. Do you know what would happen to it if I came out with a *coffee-table book?*"

"Will you stop calling it that? Forget it. Forget I said anything." After a moment she added, "I guess your work would just duplicate what's in the bookstores. I mean, it's not like plenty of well-researched, comprehensive books haven't already been written about those guys."

Cat heard something that sounded suspiciously like a snort of disdain. She bit back a self-satisfied smile.

Brody pushed himself away from the fence. "Enough lollygagging. There's work to do. Lies and sleazy innuendo to pen."

They ambled toward the parking lot. This burst of industriousness was rare for Brody. Cat was relieved to see him throw himself into his work rather than mope over the lost head-writer job.

"Didn't you already send the manuscript on Nolan Branigan off to Leon?" she asked.

"Yep. I'm starting a new project. The Demons."

"You're writing about a major league ball club?"

He nodded, placing a hand on her waist to guide her around the kiddie boat pond. "You wouldn't believe what I've dug up about the players and management."

"I probably wouldn't," she agreed. "Do you?"

His smile told her that really wasn't relevant.

She asked, "What are you going to do without me around to read the racy stuff to and watch my ears turn red?" The way he'd done with the Branigan book.

Brody's smile faded. He didn't look at her. Cat's nape prickled. She grabbed his arm, planting them both at the edge of the parking lot.

"Let me have it, Brody. Whatever it is, tell me right now or I'm not budging an inch."

He turned to her with a grin so warm and beguiling she knew she was in trouble. "I couldn't bear to part with my office mom."

"What have you done?"

"I called Nana. Hired you on for another month."

All Cat could do was gape at him.

"What?" he said. "Is it so terrible working with me? I thought this job was pretty much a plum. Later hours, you get to sleep in—"

"I never sleep in!" she hollered. Especially not now, with a queasy stomach nudging her awake. "How *could* you? You *know* how much I wanted this over with—how awkward this is for me!"

"What can I tell you?" he asked dryly. "I'm a sadist."

"Are you hoping I'll sleep with you? Is that it?" she yelled, ignoring the wide-eyed matron ushering her brood out of a nearby minivan. "Because let me tell you something. That is *not* going to happen!"

"Your devotion to Mr. Perfect is immensely heartwarming. Can we discuss this in the car?"

"There's nothing to discuss! You're not going to change your mind. You're just going to threaten me some more."

Now it was his turn to gape. "*Threaten* you!"

"You'll tell Nana about us and she'll fire me."

Brody's silence told her he was still prepared to sabotage her career. Cat stalked past him, blindly heading for his Porsche Boxster, a sleek convertible in pale metallic jade green. Brakes squealed nearby and a driver cursed her out.

Brody's voice followed her. "You act like it's *torture* working for me! What did I ever do to you?"

She turned and impaled him with an oh-come-now look.

He joined her at the car. "What, just because we slept together once, you can't get past that and—"

"Why are you doing this to me? What happened between us was a mistake, Brody."

"A *horrendous* mistake—I believe that's the way you put it."

Cat couldn't recall saying anything so insensitive, but if she had, that would account for his bitterness. Was that why he was doing this, then—to avenge his bruised pride?

He obviously assumed she didn't want to work with her "horrendous mistake" while she was supposedly in love with another man. The truth was so much more complex and confusing. Brigit had been nagging her to get a pregnancy test, and even though Cat was certain she wasn't expecting—*I'm late, is all*—she'd been inclined to humor Brigit and do it, but only after her assignment with Brody had ended and she knew she'd never have to set eyes on him again.

Because if she was wrong, and the test came out positive, and she had to face the father of her baby day after day...

Cat couldn't deal with that. Already during the past month her feelings for Brody had become much too complicated. Self-indulgent, unreliable, obsessed with a sophomoric need for negative attention, Brody Mikhailov, aka the notorious Jake Beckett, was the last man she would have chosen to father her child. He was a hack writer whose sole objective was to shock and titillate, though he possessed the talent and means to accomplish so much more.

Even so, Cat had to admit she'd begun to soften toward him, a natural result, she supposed, of their enforced togetherness. At least she'd been able to maintain some degree of objectivity, so far. But she knew that would end if she were to discover she was carrying his child. Her emotions would get the better of her. She'd start twisting things around, straining to detect redeeming qualities in the father of her child. She'd fool herself into thinking he was something he wasn't, just like so many other women who became trapped in lousy relationships because they had blinders on until it was too late.

Cat reminded herself why she'd sought an arranged pregnancy in the first place, why she'd opted for single parenthood. No child of hers was going to go through what she'd endured. Getting too close to a man like Brody Mikhailov was almost a guarantee of a broken family somewhere down the road.

She'd just have to put off the pregnancy test for another month.

If she had to have one at all. *I'm not pregnant,* she reminded herself. *I'm premenstrual!* Soon enough her body would get up to speed and provide her with proof positive that she wasn't in the family way. She wouldn't need to pee on any damn stick.

Cat opened the door and looked at Brody over the top of the sports car. "Some ground rules from here on out. No more plying me with alcohol. No more 'accidentally' groping me. No more following me around the house to read me the dirty parts of your books."

"Are you finished?"

"No." She stabbed a finger toward him. "No doing whatever it is you're thinking about right now."

"Darn."

"And I don't want to hear a peep out of you for the whole ride home, is that clear?"

"Have you thought about having a baby, Cat? I'm telling you, you'd make a hell of a mom."

"And I don't want to hear a peep out of you for a whole week. Is that clear?"

"Have you thought about buying a TV? I'm telling you, nothing...."

7

FROM HIS PERCH on a wooden bench just inside the mall, Brody scrutinized the shoppers meandering out of Macy's. As the minutes passed, his trepidation ripened into something approaching panic.

Cat had dashed into the department store in search of the ladies' room about the time she started turning an alarming shade of gray. This wasn't the first time. She'd lost her breakfast shortly after arriving at his house that morning, just as she had almost daily for the last couple of weeks, since she'd begun her second month working with him.

The first time, he'd tried to send her home, and had even offered to drive her to her doctor. She'd insisted it was something she'd eaten and that she felt all better. But then it had happened the next day, and the next, while she continued to pretend nothing was wrong.

Cat's constant fatigue was another worrisome factor. Twice during the past week she'd fallen asleep in the afternoon, once in the computer room when he'd stepped out for a minute while she'd been teaching him to balance his checkbook, and again in the kitchen. Brody had walked in to find Cat slumped over the table, her head pillowed on her arms and a panful of brownies turning to chocolate bricks in the oven.

It hadn't taken long for the inevitable suspicion to plant itself in Brody's mind. But hadn't she told him she was on the Pill? Which brought him back to the only other possibility—that she was indeed sick, with something serious enough to last several weeks.

Where *was* she? He debated going in after her. What if she'd passed out in the ladies' room? He glanced at the watch she'd insisted he purchase. One more minute. He'd give her sixty seconds and then he was going in.

Scanning the crowd, Brody caught a glimpse of wavy red hair. He leaped to his feet, knocking over two of the seven overstuffed shopping bags piled around him. He reached her in about five seconds, weaving around a power-walking elderly couple, two mothers pushing strollers, and a knot of heavily made up adolescent mall rats.

"Brody, the bags!" Cat glanced worriedly at their purchases, left unattended. Her coloring was nearly normal, he was relieved to see. She just looked tired.

"Let me worry about the bags. Are you okay?" He led her back to the bench and sat her down.

"I'm fine now. It was nothing."

He scowled down at her. "That's what you say every time, Cat. When are you going to go to the doctor?"

"I'm not sick. I must've eaten something bad

and it's just taking a while to work its way out of my system."

"Two weeks? I'm taking you to the doctor. Today. Give me the number and I'll make an appointment."

"Brody, I really don't need—"

"If you won't cooperate, I'll take you to mine."

"You have a doctor?"

After a moment he said, "No. But there are those walk-in places. Or the emergency room."

"I'm not going to the emergency room for an upset stomach!"

"You know, if you took care of yourself half as well as you take care of other people, you wouldn't be going through this now."

She looked so miserable, he pushed a bag aside and sat next to her. Quietly he said, "You know what I thought when this first started? I thought maybe you were pregnant. But then I remembered you told me you're on the Pill." She avoided his gaze, and his heartbeat picked up speed. "That's what you said, right, Cat? You're on the Pill?"

He saw her debating her response. *No. This can't happen*, he thought, as his whole body tensed. He'd been uncharacteristically careless that night, true, but at the time he'd thought she was a professional, and had assumed she'd protected herself. He hadn't bargained on a pregnancy scare, that was for damn sure!

"Cat?"

She glanced at him and pushed her hair behind her ear. "I—I was on the Pill when, you know, when we were together. You and me."

"You *were*."

She nodded, looking away.

Brody relaxed. He wiped his sweaty palms on his jeans. It wasn't his, at least. "And now?"

She took a moment to answer. "I went off it after that. Um, because of side effects."

"And you've been seeing Mr. Per—Greg this whole time."

She nodded.

"Without birth control."

She clenched her hands together. "I guess not."

Those mental images Brody had banished by force of will came hurtling back with a vengeance: Cat writhing on the sheets with her faceless lover, arching against him, taking him into her body; giving herself unreservedly to the man she loved, night after night.

Growing that man's baby in her body.

Brody glanced at Cat's belly. He should be rejoicing—another bullet dodged. This wasn't his problem. It was Cat's problem. And Mr. Perfect's.

So why did he feel like it was his problem?

He said, "Are you late?"

She nodded. "I've missed two periods."

"Two!"

"And my breasts are sore and I can't stand even looking at Brie cheese and I've always *loved* Brie cheese!"

She sat limp and listless, and Brody wondered if he'd ever seen anyone look so wretched. "Oh, honey…" He put his arm around her shoulders and said the first thing that came to mind. "It'll be okay."

"Ha ha ha," she muttered, but Brody knew he'd spoken the truth. It would be okay because Mr. Perfect would make it okay. The guy was responsible, dependable, a stand-up fellow. Hadn't she rubbed it in, all the differences between Greg and Brody? Her boyfriend wouldn't let her down. Guys like Greg Bannister had invented the phrase "do the right thing," just for this particular situation.

In no time at all, Brody's office mom would be installed in whatever passed for suburban splendor in Alaska—a cozy split-level igloo perhaps, with a two-dogsled garage and a plastic flamingo out front.

On the other side of the world, practically. Reflexively Brody pulled her closer. "I take it you haven't done a pregnancy test yet."

She shook her head. "I want to wait until…well, I just want to wait."

"No more waiting. We'll pick up one of those drugstore kits." He pulled her up off the bench.

"No."

"What do you mean, no? You've gotta find out."

"I will," she said, "when I'm ready."

"Well, I'm ready now. Is there a pharmacy in this place?"

He shooed away her hands when she tried to lift a bag, and grabbed the handles of all seven himself. They were awkward to carry and much too heavy for a mother-to-be, filled with a wrought-iron magazine rack, black marble bookends and other household furnishings that reflected the taste of the homeowner in question, which was to say, a heterosexual male. After Cat's fourth unsolicited offer to help him redecorate, he'd figured he'd have to give in or risk having her wonder just why he was so attached to floral chintz and white eyelet.

They'd ordered furniture earlier in the week and picked out new paint and wallpaper. Cat had suggested he have the pastel carpeting taken up and the hardwood floors refinished. After years of stolid indifference, he found he was actually looking forward to living in a home that suited his own tastes.

BRODY POUNDED ON THE DOOR of the upstairs bathroom. "What's taking so long?"

"Leave me alone!"

"Need some help?"

"I don't need help! Now, leave me alone!"

"Touchy," he muttered, leaving his post by the door to wrestle with Spot.

Several minutes later the bathroom door opened and Cat emerged, looking pale and dazed.

"Where's the, uh, thingamajig?" he asked.

She nodded toward the bathroom. He went in and examined the white plastic wand. He knew what the plus sign meant; he'd read the instructions aloud to her.

"Okay. So now you know." He turned to see the hallway empty. "Cat?"

Brody looked in each room as he hurried

down the hall. "Cat!" He sprinted down the stairs, calling out, "Come on, we'll deal with this. We'll get through it. Cat?" He peered out the front windows, relieved to see her car in the driveway, wondering where this "we" stuff was coming from.

This isn't your problem, he reminded himself. *Leave the hand-holding to the boyfriend.*

The hand-holding and everything that went with it: the lovemaking, the nest building, the child rearing, the growing old together. Cat and her Mr. Perfect.

"Where is she, boy?" he asked the dog, who was whining by the back door. Brody let him out, startled to see Cat sitting calmly at the picnic table, flipping through a magazine.

He watched her for a few moments before taking a seat across from her. She glanced up at him and asked, "Are you going to barbecue those salmon steaks tonight? I wouldn't keep them for another day."

"I thought I would, yes."

"I'll pick up some corn. Maybe I'll cook it on the coals."

Brody propped his elbows on the table. "We're going to talk about this, Cat."

Her neutral expression never faltered. "No offense, Brody, but it really doesn't affect you."

An unwelcome thought jabbed him. Slowly he straightened. "You're not thinking of getting rid of it."

"No!" Her icy reserve evaporated in a heartbeat. "I'd never do that. I *want* this baby!" She clamped her lips shut, having clearly revealed more than she'd intended.

"That's okay, honey. It's okay to want your baby. Just because it wasn't planned doesn't mean..." He reached across the table and captured her icy hand. He threaded his fingers through hers. "You've got to tell Greg right away."

He saw her swallow convulsively. She studied the magazine spread open in front of her. It was *People*, which he subscribed to for business reasons—to help stay abreast of who was saying what about whom. Cat hated *People*.

"I'll...tell him." Her voice was so faint, he had to strain to make out her words.

"Tonight," he said. "Or now. You can call him from here."

"No! No, in person. I'll see him."

"Tonight, Cat. He should know, he should be taking care of you now." Brody rubbed his thumb on the soft skin of her hand. "It's his responsibility."

She looked at him, a question in her shimmering eyes. He wished he could read her mind. She opened her mouth to speak, then simply sagged, like a deflated balloon.

"You didn't expect this, did you?" he asked. "You should have, you know. Two missed periods, the nausea..."

"I didn't want it to be true."

"Denial."

She gave him a tired little smile. "That's what my friend Brigit said."

"This is the same Brigit who bought you that

negligee?'' he asked. Cat had wanted to make it
clear she hadn't chosen the scandalous thing
herself. Foolish woman.

"Yep."

"This Brigit sounds like a very sensible
woman. Bring her around sometime. I'd like to
meet her." Even though she was Greg's cousin,
if he remembered correctly.

With a watery chuckle, Cat said, "I don't
think you're ready for Brigit. Most people
aren't."

"I mean it, Cat." He pinned her with his stern-
est glare. "You're going to tell him. Tonight."

8

"I TOLD HIM," Cat said, before he could ask. She dropped her purse on a living room chair. Her stomach was doing its morning pitch and roll. "Did the floor guy get back to you?"

"And...?" Brody gestured impatiently.

"You want me to relate our whole private conversation?" She tried to walk past him, but he blocked her way.

"Yes. Don't leave anything out."

"Sorry to disappoint you, but that's between Greg and me." She shook him off and started for the kitchen. "I hope you still have those saltines."

"I bought three more boxes for you," he said, following her. "And a gallon of milk."

She pulled the box of crackers out of a cabinet. "You bought me milk? Why?"

"Aren't pregnant women supposed to drink milk?"

"I don't know. I've never been pregnant before."

"This is the sort of thing you're supposed to ask your doctor. Have you made an appointment?"

"Will you stop it?" she griped around a mouthful of cracker. "I'm the one who's supposed to nag, remember? *I'm* being paid to take care of *you*."

Brody reached into the refrigerator for the milk. "Did you set a date?"

"I don't have an appointment yet. I haven't even chosen—"

"No, a date for the wedding."

The saltine in Cat's hand broke in two.

He added, "Unless you want to waddle down the aisle in a white satin tent, I suggest you hurry it up."

"Who said we're getting married?"

Brody gaped at her as most of the milk he was pouring ended up on the counter. "Of course you're getting married!"

"I don't recall saying any such thing."

"But he asked you, right? I mean, Greg wants to marry you."

She shoved her hair behind her ears and crossed her arms. "We didn't discuss marriage."

Brody held his palms up, as if staving off this latest complication. "No no. That's not the way this works. The guy got you *pregnant*, Cat. He's supposed to *marry* you."

"He's *supposed* to? This is practically the twenty-first century, Brody. I'm a grown woman, self-sufficient. It doesn't have to work that way."

Brody's color had spiked. "He's supposed to *do the right thing!*" he declared, slapping the counter for emphasis.

Cat was momentarily speechless. Finally she asked, "Would you?"

"What?"

"Would you…do the right thing? If you got a woman pregnant?"

His telling pause was answer enough. Cat was sorry she'd asked, even before he said, "Thank God I've never had to find out."

She'd thought the crackers had settled her queasy stomach. Now she wasn't so sure.

He said, "You're trying to dodge the issue, and it won't work. This isn't about me, it's about the guy who did this to you. Where's he staying? I'm gonna go straighten him out."

"No! This is nuts, Brody. Listen to yourself!"

"His name is Greg Bannister, right? Just give me the name of his hotel. Or is he staying with Brigit?"

"I don't *want* to get married!"

He gave her a yeah-right look. "If the father of your unborn child got down on bended knee, you'd want it. Your pride is keeping you from admitting it—"

"Oh God…" She leaned back against the counter, dropped her head into her hands.

"—But deep down, it's what you want, what you and the baby need."

After a few moments Brody came to her and gently lifted her face. His expression was heart-breakingly sincere. "He doesn't deserve you, Cat. He doesn't deserve someone as warm and giving and bighearted as you."

She couldn't have responded if she'd tried, couldn't have gotten words past the knot of emotion in her throat.

His thumbs caressed her cheeks. A gentle

smile touched his eyes. "Maybe the news just freaked him out. He'll come around."

She pulled in a shaky breath and eased away from him. "It doesn't matter, Brody. I'm prepared to raise my child alone."

"You shouldn't have to—"

"Having one parent isn't the worst thing that can happen to a child." She lowered herself into a chair, feeling wearier than she could ever remember.

Brody placed the glass of milk in front of Cat, then stood gripping the back of the chair across from her. "But it's also not the best. Every child deserves a real home."

She stiffened. "My child will have a real—"

"With two parents."

"I had two parents. Believe me, I wish I hadn't."

Brody absorbed that for a moment, then pulled out the chair and slid into it.

Cat held up her hand. "I didn't mean to get into that."

"Tell me."

She already knew there was no use trying to keep something from Brody Mikhailov, aka Jake Beckett, aka the King of Sling. If he wanted to, he could probably make a phone call or two and find out where Jimmy Hoffa was.

She looked longingly at the full coffeemaker, filling the kitchen with its irresistible perfume.

"Not for you," he said, shoving the milk under her nose. "And no more wine, either. And if anything has to be lifted, you wait for me."

She glared. "Are you going to be doing this for the next two and a half weeks?"

"Doing what? Making sure you look after yourself? And your baby?"

Your baby. Cat felt a sudden tightness in her chest. "I don't need you badgering me."

"Yeah, right. You wouldn't even know you're pregnant if I hadn't bought the damn test and made you use it. Drink your milk."

"You poured me too much." She took a swallow.

"So. Your folks. What's the story?" When she gave him a disgruntled look he added, "Hey, I came clean with you. I told you stuff I never told anyone. You're not allowed to hold back."

She wasn't going to win this one. "It's a common story, really. No big deal. My parents divorced."

"How old were you?"

"Eight."

"That's a rough age to go through something like that."

"Is there a good age?"

He leaned back. "Do you have siblings?"

She shook her head. "Mom and Dad despised each other for as long as I can remember, since well before they split. There was this horrible custody battle. Even then I knew it wasn't because they wanted me, it was just to hurt each other."

"They were using you."

Now that she'd started talking about it, the memories wouldn't let her stop. "They spent all their money on the lawyers, just trying to wear

each other down. Even after the judge warned
them that a trial would eat up all their assets,
they refused to settle. It was more important to
destroy each other than to salvage what they
could. In the end there was nothing left, not
even the house."

Brody remained silent, and for that, Cat was
grateful. She'd never gotten over it, she realized.
She still lived with the pain and confusion of
those early years. Her parents' raw, undisguised
hatred had spilled over onto her. Even now, she
felt tainted by it.

"So you see," she finally said, her voice shaky,
"I know from firsthand experience. Sometimes
it's better to have one loving parent than…than
the alternative."

Brody fiddled with the pepper mill, ignoring
the black grindings sprinkling the table. "You
talk as if divorce is the only alternative. Is that
what you think? That you and Greg wouldn't be
able to make it work?"

"Look at the statistics."

"The statistics also show a lot of couples staying together, Cat."

"What made you such a big fan of wedded
bliss?" she asked, and immediately recalled
his own miserable childhood. Chagrined, she
added, "Okay. There are worse things than being from a broken family. But, Brody, you have
to admit, I'm not…I'm not like your mother."

"No. You're not. And your child will never go
through what I did. For that matter, if you and
the baby's father did marry, and did end up divorcing, you wouldn't turn it into a horror show

the way your folks did. Most divorces are civilized. Even amicable—that's the word you always hear."

Cat hadn't thought of it that way. He was right. If she ever divorced, she'd consider the children first. Things would never get that out of control.

"Your parents were selfish and small-minded," he said. "Is Greg like that?"

"I don't… No, of course not."

Brody tossed his hand, as if to say *I rest my case.*

Cat said, "You're really eager to marry me off to him, aren't you?" She didn't know who she was more peeved with—Brody for throwing her at her fictional lover, or herself for caring.

He scanned the countertop as a muscle near his eye twitched. "I just feel a child needs two committed parents whenever possible."

"Are you looking for your cigarettes? I think I see them on top of the fridge. What are they doing up there?"

"I forgot. I put them there to remind me not to smoke around you."

"Brody, this is your house! You have a right to—"

"Now you *want* me to smoke?"

"I didn't say that! Of course I don't want you to smoke!"

"Then what's the problem?"

Arguing with Brody was exhausting, and she had no energy to spare. "Do what you want," she muttered, then remembered the painters were due to start upstairs today. "Weren't you going to clear off the dining table so you can work there?''

"I postponed the painting for a few weeks."

"Why? I thought you were eager to get the place finished."

"The paint fumes. You shouldn't be inhaling them."

"Good grief, Brody, you can't rearrange your entire life around my pregnancy.... Of course, there is a solution. We could call it quits now. You could tell Nana you didn't need me as long as you'd thought."

He studied her so intently, Cat had to break eye contact. "You really hate this, don't you?" he asked softly. "Working with me."

"It's not that." Conflicting impulses bombarded Cat: the urge to run away and safeguard her secret; and the almost overwhelming need to blurt out the truth, as well as the futile, foolhardy yearnings of her heart. *You're going to be a father. Stay with me. Stay and watch our child grow.*

Even if she told him the baby was his, the fact remained that Brody didn't want to be a father. He'd admitted that he wouldn't necessarily "do the right thing" himself, though he expected Greg to. She supposed she should be thankful for his candor.

"This assignment is just uncomfortable for me," she said. "You know that. And you know why."

Brody kept his gaze directed at the pepper mill, which he was lining up just so next to the salt shaker. "I thought things had kind of changed between us, these last few weeks." He glanced at his hands, grubby with ground pepper, and wiped them on his jeans. "I mean, I thought we've been getting along pretty well."

He was right. Things had indeed changed between them. They'd spent every weekday together for the past month and a half, working, eating, running errands, sometimes just shooting the breeze. Practically living together. They'd begun to connect on a fundamental level. Cat had tried to tell herself it was inevitable, the result of enforced togetherness, but she could no longer fool herself. It was more than that.

She'd be lying if she claimed she didn't enjoy Brody's company, even looked forward to it on the long drive from Tarrytown each morning. To call it an uncomfortable arrangement was laughable. But neither of them was laughing. In different circumstances, she could fall in love with Brody Mikhailov. The thought terrified her.

In truth, she needed to get away from Brody *because of* their growing closeness—not because she was uncomfortable with him but because she was too comfortable. It felt too good being with him, too right. Her future and her child's depended on following through with her original plan. The King of Sling had done his part, albeit unwittingly. In two and a half weeks she had to walk away and never look back.

Cat met his gaze resolutely, while her hands clenched in her lap around fistfuls of her white cotton sundress. "Don't ask Nana to extend my service with you again, Brody. If you do, I'll refuse. If that means I lose my job, so be it."

A desolate shadow touched his eyes, fleetingly, before his features hardened. Cat was reminded of the defenseless child he'd been, shunned and neglected, and forced herself not to look away. Receiving this kind of blunt rejection from his office mom had to trigger unwanted memories of his real mother.

"Don't worry," he said, rising. His sullen gaze lit briefly on the pack of cigarettes on top of the refrigerator, but he didn't reach for them. "I'll give you a glowing recommendation. Your job is safe, but for how long? Have you decided what you're going to do when Nana realizes her favorite employee isn't the vestal virgin she thought?"

"I...haven't gotten that far. I'll get something—some kind of job—till the baby comes."

"But how long can you—" He broke off, then shoved his chair under the table with more force than necessary, making her jump. "Like you said, it's your business. But if I were in your shoes, I'd be making sure the kid's father lived up to his responsibility. That's all I'm going to say about it."

9

BRODY WAS AS GOOD as his word. Over the next nine days, he restrained the overwhelming urge to challenge Cat about her maddeningly nebulous future plans. Instead, he made sure she ate right and relaxed with her feet up every afternoon. He badgered her until she saw an obstetrician, who pronounced her pregnancy normal and free of complications.

He had central air-conditioning installed to make her last couple of weeks with him more comfortable. Even if he never turned it on after she left, the expression on her face when she stepped out of the August swelter into his glacial living room made it worth every penny.

The cigarettes stayed on the fridge, the vodka stayed in the freezer and the coffee carafe stayed empty—from noon to eight, anyway, when his office mom was in residence. Cat accused him of being overprotective, but *somebody* had to look after her!

His pack-a-day cigarette habit had been whittled down to a handful of smokes, one or two in the morning before she arrived, and the rest late at night while he worked on *Demonic!*, the book about the Demons baseball team that would expose its crooked and carnal underbelly to the glaring light of public scrutiny, and make an entire major league ball club and its millions of fans mad as hell at him.

Let them do their worst. He'd rather face an army of large and powerful, tobacco-spitting, crotch-grabbing, baseball-bat-wielding professional athletes than one more nightmare featuring that morgue shot of Serena Milton.

Brody had to admit, though, that his heart wasn't in *Demonic!*, and not only because the bulk of his "facts" came courtesy of jilted groupies, ambitious rookie rivals and embittered ex-wives. His taste for mudslinging had waned in recent weeks; he found he no longer had the stomach for it. The notoriety he'd once craved had begun to lose its seductive allure.

Not that he would ever allow his newfound aversion to undermine his career. As he'd told Cat, he had a reputation to protect—and to cash in on. No coffee-table tomes for him yet.

Lately, however, he felt increasingly detached from his professional persona of Jake Beckett. It was as if, in his own mind at least, Brody had begun to distance himself from his infamous alter ego, the hack writer unencumbered by scruples or lofty aspirations.

Jake Beckett had become more than Brody Mikhailov's pen name; he'd become a separate and distinct personality, whose corrosive mindset Brody had to actively call forth every time he sat down to work on *Demonic!*

He heard the shower start upstairs and deliberately tormented himself with the mental image of Cat rinsing beach sand off her body—that lovely body he'd know in the dark but which he'd never seen.

From his reclining position on the living room sofa, flipping through the latest issue of *Cineaste*, Brody gazed at the ceiling and imagined his office mom standing under the warm spray, rubbing herself all over to shed the fine white sand, paying special attention to those delightful nooks and crannies he remembered in graphic detail.

When he'd told her to bring a swimsuit today for an excursion to Jones Beach, his overactive imagination had conjured an abbreviated tigerstripe bikini, thong style. Naturally, she'd opted for a sensible, dark green one-piece, but he hadn't been able to keep his eyes off her.

He'd had Cat rub sunscreen all over him, of course, but the only place she'd permitted him to return the favor was on the scant square inches of her back not covered by the racer-style suit. The rest she'd done herself.

Brody had already showered and thrown on a pair of denim shorts. He laid the magazine facedown on his bare chest, listening to the murmur of water in the old pipes, still staring at the ceiling. He supposed the fact that Cat was pregnant—with another man's child, no less—should be a sexual turnoff, but it wasn't. Perhaps that would change when she started to show. Then he remembered that he wouldn't get to see her become big with child. He'd never see her again after next week.

A strange heaviness weighed him down. Even though Mr. Perfect had turned into Mr.

Deadbeat, Cat was still crazy about him. Why else would she be so dead set against extending her assignment with Brody? He was her "horrendous mistake" in the flesh—a constant reminder of how she'd unwittingly betrayed the jerk she was in love with.

Brody could call her bluff, of course, and try to rehire her for another month, another three months, a year. Would she really dig in her heels, as she'd threatened, and refuse to continue working with him? Probably. She was just bullheaded enough to spill the beans to Nana herself, in order to beat Brody to the punch.

Not that he'd tell Nana a damn thing about that night in the agency's apartment. At one time he would have, without a qualm, but no longer. He couldn't do that to Cat, and not just because she'd lose her job. He hated to think how excruciatingly embarrassed she would be to have her respected employer find out what she'd done.

Of course, Cat didn't know his threat had no teeth. And he intended to keep it that way; her fear of being fired was all that kept her from walking out of his home and out of his life, at least for the next week.

And after next week? As Brody pondered what it might take to keep her with him through the fall, and perhaps the winter as well, the answer whacked him on the head, just as the shower was turned off upstairs. Okay, he was still a selfish bastard, but at least he'd gone from coercion to harmless manipulation.

A muffled thud interrupted his thoughts, followed by a sharp cry. He was upstairs and down the hall before he knew he was moving. "Cat!" He slammed his fist on the bathroom door. "What happened?"

Brody didn't wait for a response, but threw open the door. Through the scented steam and foggy glass of the tub enclosure he saw she was doubled over. "Cat!" He hauled the sliding glass door aside.

Cat jerked up, releasing the foot she'd been clutching. "Brody!" She tried to close the door, but he wouldn't release it. "Get out of here!"

"Are you hurt?" He made a grab for her foot, but she yanked it away.

"Hand me my towel!" she demanded. Whatever mishap Cat had suffered, it wasn't enough to override her outraged modesty.

He stopped and looked at her then, really looked at her. She stood in the tub soaking wet, stark naked and scowling murderously. She made no attempt to cover herself with her hands, but simply stood there, arms at her sides, waiting for Brody to miraculously turn into a gentleman and offer her the towel.

"Oh, Cat..." A slow smile stretched his face. "Honey, you are so beautiful."

Her scowl faltered. He watched a range of emotions dance in her crystalline eyes. Now her hands came up, tentatively, to shield herself from his view. He seized them gently, held them out at her sides.

She had a redhead's pale skin, slightly pink from the sun everywhere her suit hadn't covered her, despite the sunblock she'd slathered on. Her body didn't conform to the prevailing ideals of female beauty. She was neither boyish nor butch: her ribs didn't show; her muscles weren't defined. But to him she was perfect, all soft, seductive curves. All woman.

She took his breath away.

Cat tugged against him, but he only tightened his grip. Wavy tendrils of wet hair clung to her face. "Brody. Let me go."

Instead, he pulled her out of the tub, belatedly recalling why he'd barged into the john in the first place. He looked at her foot as she reached for the blue-and-white-striped towel she'd placed on the vanity.

"What did you do?" he asked.

She wrapped the towel around herself. "I dropped the shampoo bottle on my foot when I went to put it back on the shelf."

The bottle was heavy, the tub shelf high. "Ouch." He sat her down on the toilet lid and squatted to examine her foot. A red spot had already blossomed on the instep, heralding the nasty bruise to come. Tenderly he cradled her foot, massaged it.

"It's nothing," Cat said. Her voice quavered slightly.

He looked past her foot, to her rosy calves and knees, to her glistening thighs and the mysterious shadow between. The damp towel barely covered her hips, barely concealed the lush triangle he now knew to be dark auburn. She clutched the towel tighter to her breasts.

Brody looked into her eyes. He read her turmoil. He felt the haunting drumbeat of memories like a shared pulse. His hand curled around her ankle and she flinched.

Quietly he said, "You owe him nothing."

She parted her lips to speak; the words died in her throat.

"Nothing," he repeated, burning his gaze into hers. He shifted closer to her, resting one knee on the floor tiles. He propped her foot on his thigh and stroked his fingers up the back of her calf.

Her mouth quivered, but the only plea came from her eyes.

"You'll have to say it, Cat." His fingertips traced the moist crease at the back of her knee. "If you want me to stop, you'll have to tell me."

Cat closed her eyes, and opened them slowly. She held the towel closed with one hand and reached down to grasp his wrist with the other, which didn't keep him from lightly fondling the back of her raised thigh. Her breath caught.

"You want me to stop?" he asked. "Say the word. I'll stop."

He felt a grim satisfaction watching her struggle with her conflicting emotions. She hadn't given everything to Mr. Perfect. She'd held a little piece of herself back, and that little piece called to him like a Siren.

"You think about it, don't you?" he asked, still caressing her. "That night. What we did in the dark. You don't want to, but you do."

A ragged sigh escaped her. She released his wrist. "It never should have happened."

It was the party line, but this time it lacked conviction. Brody smiled. "You think about it when you're alone." He slid his hand along her inner thigh. She looked away. "What do you do then?" he asked. "Do you touch yourself?"

"Brody..." She sounded out of breath.

He felt her fine tremors, inhaled her soapy, womanly scent. His fingers disappeared under the towel. They brushed past damp hair to the slippery, swollen petals. Cat made a guttural sound as if in pain. Brody cupped her face with his free hand and made her look at him. Her eyes were slumberous, her mouth half-open.

"Do you touch yourself like this?" He probed a little deeper and found her wet opening. "When you think about that night?"

Her knuckles were white where she clasped the towel. He moved his finger higher, to the taut little heart of sensation. She gasped. Her thighs fell open, and the last vestige of his restraint splintered.

Brody was only dimly aware of lifting Cat, perching her on the edge of the vanity and wrenching the towel off her. His urgency had teeth. It was as if his next breath depended on being inside her.

He opened her legs wide and positioned himself between them even as he kicked away his own clothing. Cat wrapped her limbs around him, panting softly. He widened his stance, steadied her and plunged to the hilt in one sure, deep stroke. She sobbed her pleasure, clutching him, arching against him. Her inner muscles clenched him and he groaned, struggling against the explosive imminence of his orgasm.

Brody grabbed the towel and wiped condensation off the wall-to-wall vanity mirror behind her. Their first time had been in impenetrable darkness. Now he had an unobstructed view of every inch of her, front and back.

Mesmerized, he watched himself slowly withdraw, as Cat clutched at him, whimpering. Just as slowly he pressed into her slick heat and lifted his gaze to her flushed face.

"I knew you were lovely, that night, but I didn't know..." He smiled in wonder. "I didn't know you were perfect."

He set a languid rhythm, which she met with supple undulations. Had she looked like this that night, when he couldn't see her? Had her expression been this endearingly open and unguarded? Had her eyes conveyed this heady potpourri of emotions? Euphoria. Vulnerability. Trust.

If he'd been able to see her that night, he might have fallen in love with her right then and there.

Brody hauled her close and tucked his face into the crook of her neck. His heart galloped with the realization, even as his rational mind disavowed it.

She belonged to another man. She was carrying another man's child. Brody had no right to love her.

As if she sensed his agitation, Cat held him tight. She stroked his hair and pressed her lips to his temple. Brody turned his head and captured her mouth in a desperate kiss, painfully aware that this physical joining, this pure and fleeting oneness of body, was all he dared ask for, hope for.

As they rocked together, he watched Cat's gaze focus inward, felt her restless impatience as her passion mounted. He delighted in her breathless cries, in the ferocity with which she clung to him as her shuddering climax began to overtake her. Her eyes squeezed shut.

"Look at me," he whispered, willing her to open herself to him absolutely. Her lids fluttered; her luminous gaze locked on his.

"Brody…" she whispered, and smiled, and fell apart in his arms. He felt it, stoked it, until the violence of his own release consumed him.

And even then, he never took his eyes from hers.

10

"YOU HAVE NO REASON to feel guilty, you know."

Brody's words were a warm buzz against Cat's scalp. Clad in nothing but a thin sheet, the two of them cuddled spoon fashion in his bed, his chest to her back. The air-conditioning was off and the windows stood open to late afternoon sunshine that slanted into the sleeping alcove and across the old-fashioned four-poster bed.

The summer-scented breeze, postcoital lethargy and the solid comfort of Brody's strong arms around her lulled Cat like a narcotic. If she'd ever felt this tranquil, she couldn't remember.

He gave her shoulder a little shake. "Did you hear me?"

"Who says I feel guilty?"

"He doesn't deserve fidelity." When she didn't respond, Brody rose on an elbow and brushed strands of damp hair off her face. His fingertips were slightly rough. They felt wonderful. "I don't want you beating yourself up over this."

"I don't want to talk about it."

Cat sensed him debating the wisdom of pursuing the issue, before he settled behind her once more. She felt his steady heartbeat and the measured rise and fall of his broad chest. The angular swaths of sunlight lengthened, crept snail-like over the hills and valleys of their sheet-draped forms. Cat had begun to drift off when Brody spoke again.

"I'd marry you myself if I didn't know you and the baby are better off without me."

The bleak certainty in his voice made her eyes burn with unshed tears. She caressed his arm draped over her torso. "You're very hard on yourself, Brody."

She felt his trademark smile as he nuzzled her hair. "I try not to be blind to my own shortcomings. There are only one or two of them, but they're doozies."

Cat tried to look over her shoulder at him. "Is that why you've never married? Because you feel—what? Unworthy? Like you wouldn't be a fit parent?"

"Not everyone's cut out for it. They should leave the job to people who know how to do it right." His hand slid down to Cat's belly. His touch was cherishing, almost reverent. Brody's unquestioning faith in her mothering ability sent a rush of pride through her. She placed her hand over his.

"For the record," she said, when she could speak around the lump in her throat, "I think you'd probably figure out how to do it right."

"Does that mean you accept? Should I book a wedding band?"

Though she knew Brody's proposal was in

jest, Cat sensed a hopeful undercurrent in his voice, and in the way he tensed, almost imperceptibly, awaiting her response. It was her imagination, of course. Brody Mikhailov was the poster boy for confirmed bachelorhood. She knew she should leave it at that, but she couldn't. She turned onto her back, still snuggled against him.

"Why do you assume you're not cut out for parenthood?" she asked. "Is it what you went through as a kid?"

He leaned up on his elbow and propped his head on his palm. "We're all a product of our upbringing. Mine didn't include any role models for how to be a good daddy."

"Brody, my parents weren't exactly Ozzie and Harriet. Yet you seem convinced I'll make a good mother."

His grin tugged at her heart. "Honey, you've got this classic, ferocious maternal instinct. You're a natural."

"I've never changed a diaper in my life."

"So?"

"I'm terrified. I'll probably faint the first time I have to give the baby a bath."

His smile turned tender and teasing at once. "Why do I think you'll get the hang of it in record time?"

"Who taught you how to bathe Spot?"

That prompted a gust of laughter. "There's nothing to hosing down a dog."

"As if you 'hosed down' that pampered mutt. I've seen you, Brody. We're talking a whole damn spa treatment. The flea check. The nail clipping. The ear cleaning. The precise water temperature. The special shampoo. And all that brushing!"

"No sense having an animal if you're going to neglect it," he grumbled.

"And all those trips to the vet. You're like an anxious parent."

"It's a dog! It's not the same thing."

She turned to face him, mimicking his posture with her head braced on her hand. "Then what about me?"

"What about you?"

"To say you've been solicitous of my condition would be the understatement of the year. You hold me through the bouts of nausea. You won't let me lift anything heavier than a pencil. You've bought me books on everything from natural childbirth to baby names. That liver you cooked me last night weighed more than my head."

"You need the B vitamins and folic acid."

Her smile was crooked. "If I didn't know better, I'd say you're acting downright nurturing."

"You can't compare that to taking care of a baby, a brand-new, helpless human being."

"Didn't I say something like that when you told me I'd make a great mother because I'm a good office mom? In the beginning, I think everyone's afraid of the responsibility of parenthood—or in awe of it, anyway. It's probably a healthy attitude. Keeps you on your toes."

He regarded her intently. "I appreciate the vote of confidence, but we both know what kind of father I'd make."

Did they? Brody had been living in his skin for forty years. He knew himself and his failings far better than she. What was she doing?

Cat flopped onto her back again. She was leaping headlong into the very trap she'd been so anxious to avoid. Trying to convince not just herself, but the father of her unborn child that he had what it took to be a good dad. For no better reason than that he'd unknowingly provided half the genes.

It was becoming harder and harder to stick to her guns, with Brody coddling her, practically reorganizing his entire household around her needs. No one had ever been so sweetly attentive to her.

And now that she'd given in and made love with him again...

Thank goodness she only had one week left.

"Maybe I..." She stared at the ceiling. "Maybe I just hate to admit some people are a lost cause. I like to think anyone can be a good parent if they just want it badly enough."

She didn't look at him. When he finally spoke, his voice was flat. "Yeah, well, I wanted to be an astronaut when I was a kid, but that's not going to happen, either."

Some things aren't meant to be. Cat repeated the adage to herself, but it did nothing to ease the aching emptiness.

He stroked her brow, smoothing the lines of tension. "You might be interested to know that I came up with a way for you to keep your job."

She looked at him.

"All during your pregnancy," he said. "And

after—as long as you want it. You could even bring the baby to work with you."

"Why is my uh-oh alarm screaming at me right now?"

"Nana wouldn't dare fire you if I insisted on keeping you on. Indefinitely."

"Brody..."

"She wouldn't even have to find out about the baby."

"We have regular staff meetings," she said. "I have to show up."

"Well, it doesn't matter. Your boss might be puritanical, but she's not going to give you the boot when she's got a well-heeled client who just can't live without his office mom. And anyway, I'm betting she'll do a little arithmetic and finger me as the likely culprit. She might figure if she lets your dastardly seducer keep you around, sooner or later he'll make an honest woman of you."

Cat sat up, pulling the sheet to her chest. "I warned you not to try this, Brody."

He sat up, too, resting a forearm on his raised knee. His playful expression turned wary. "I'm just throwing this out as an idea, Cat. That's all."

"You won't arrange it behind my back?"

Something died behind his eyes. "No. And don't worry, I won't bring it up again." He got out of bed. Shafts of sunlight skated up his body, gilding each perfect part of him in turn as he moved out of the sleeping alcove. He kept his back to her as he started to pull on his clothes.

"Brody, I..." How could she make him under-

stand, without revealing too much? "It's not that
I don't want to be here."

His chuckle held no warmth. "Honey, you
haven't wanted to be here from day one."

"But it's not you." She hugged her knees. "I
mean, it is, in a way. This is difficult for me."

He zipped his shorts. "Because of that SOB
who knocked you up."

Cat recoiled from the coarse words, and the
venom behind them. She didn't have the heart
to compound the lies at this point, so she said
nothing.

"You must really be head over heels for the
guy, to walk away from a cushy gig like this."
He tugged a white polo shirt over his head and
turned to face her. "But maybe you have a point.
As long as you stay on here, you're going to
keep cheating on Mr. Perfect. We both want it,
and God knows I'm not noble enough to keep
my hands off you."

THE DOORBELL, and Spot's howling accompaniment, roused Brody from a dead stupor the next
morning. Flaming arrows perforated his brain
just behind his eye sockets as he forced his lids
open and squinted at his sunlit surroundings.

The computer room. At some point in the wee
hours, he'd conked out on the freshly sanded
and polyurethaned hardwood floor, cradling a
half-empty bottle of vodka and a paperback
called *The Complete Guide to Breast-feeding*. He
rolled to the side and managed to overturn the
ashtray with his shoulder. Fine ash and

squashed butts pelted his face and his rumpled white shirt.

The racket downstairs escalated as a heavy fist shook the front door and Spot responded with a frenzy of barking. Brody's "Shut the hell up!" came out as a croak.

He staggered to his feet and had to grab the floor lamp when the room dipped and rolled. He struggled to locate the digital clock and bring it into focus: 10:17 a.m. Who would be pounding on his door at this ungodly hour?

Sleeping on the hard floor had effectively battered those parts of him the vodka had neglected. Every molecule of his body shrieked with pain as he hobbled down the stairs. Passing the living room, he glanced at the ornate mirror hanging over the mantel and caught a glimpse of his reflection.

Oh yeah, he thought. *There's a real Hallmark image.*

Brody opened the door to the enclosed porch. "Get out of here," he growled to Spot, who offered a compromise by parking his butt on the carpet. "I said get out." Brody pointed to the back of the house. "Go."

Spot did his classic fake-out, pretending to retreat only until his master's back was turned. Brody didn't pursue the issue. He'd never raised a hand to Spot, and it was about fourteen years too late to start now.

He yanked open the front door. *"What?"*

The stranger on his doorstep didn't so much as flinch. He was a good-looking guy about Brody's age and nearly as tall, with long, dark hair loosely tied back at the nape. He wore a white-and-black T-shirt that read Instant Human—Just Add Coffee, baggy chino shorts and brown leather sandals. He stood casually with his hands shoved in his pockets, jingling change or keys or something. To Brody it sounded like steel drums.

The guy gave Brody a quick once-over, seemingly unperturbed by the sleep-matted hair, squinty, bloodshot eyes, two-day beard stubble, ashtray effluvia and obviously slept-in clothes.

"Rough night?"

"Go away." Brody tried to close the door, but his visitor's unimpeded reflexes won out. The fellow braced the door open with a brawny arm. Spot, ever vigilant, sniffed his new friend's pockets, looking for doggie treats.

The man asked, "Are you Brody Mikhailov?"

"In the flesh." Brody patted his empty pockets. "You got a smoke on you?"

"My name's Greg Bannister."

It took a moment.

Mr. Perfect.

Shit. Now I'm gonna get my ass kicked. Thank God he was still a little drunk.

Cat must have confessed all to her boyfriend, letting her conscience overrule her common sense. Brody backed up into the porch, palms raised. "Listen, man, I just want to say one thing. Just hear me out a second."

Bannister stepped inside, letting the front door swing shut behind him. Spot leaped on him in welcome and was rewarded with a brisk head rub. "Sit, boy," Bannister said. "Good dog." Spot lifted a paw without being asked, and Bannister shook it. He glanced around the cluttered porch before letting his unreadable gaze fall once more on Brody. "I'm listening."

"It was all my fault. I want you to know that. You want to wipe the floor with me, I can't blame you. But don't take it out on Cat."

Bannister stuck his hands in his pockets, which Brody took as a hopeful sign. "Go on."

Brody shoved his fingers through his spiky hair. He reread his visitor's T-shirt. "Uh...how about I put on a pot of coffee?"

"Why not? I could use a cup."

Brody led the way, wondering if he was about to find out how it felt to get garroted. When he made it to the kitchen intact, he began to think he might actually get off easy.

Spot sprawled in the corner he favored as Brody opened the canister of coffee and began scooping grounds into the filter basket. "How much did she tell you?"

Cat's boyfriend lounged in a chair and started playing with the pepper mill, looking so at home Brody almost wished the guy would take the first swing. "I think I'd like to hear about it from you."

So. Mr. Perfect was comparing stories, ferreting out lies, inconsistencies. Cat had no doubt provided a full and honest accounting, in an effort to unburden herself of her guilt and shame.

Brody flipped the switch on the coffeemaker and grabbed a couple of mugs out of a cabinet. "Well, I guess she told you it was a, uh, kind of a comedy of errors. The first time."

Bannister leaned back in his chair, all ears.

"The thing is," Brody continued, "she never meant to cheat on you. But it was dark. Because of the blackout. So she thought I was you." He couldn't believe how lame the truth sounded. Why should Bannister believe such an outlandish story? The two of them didn't even look that much alike. "So the first time was this crazy case of mistaken identity. Milk and sugar?"

"Black. And the second time?"

Brody reeled on him, stabbing his finger for emphasis. "Now, the second time was *your* fault!"

Even hungover and half-drunk, he realized he'd probably just earned himself a mouthful of broken teeth, for starters, but Bannister merely asked, "My fault?"

Brody spread his arms. "If you'd just done the right thing, she probably would've quit her job and gone off with you to Alaska and it never would've happened again."

"The right thing?"

"If you'd married her! So the second time was your fault, buddy."

"And the third time?"

Was this a trick question? "There hasn't been a third time." *Not yet, you bastard.*

"And you think I should marry her?"

Hell no! "Hell yes!"

"I don't know...." Bannister rubbed his jaw, deep in thought. "First there's that mistaken-identity thing. And then that second time. What would you do? In my place?"

Brody's vocal cords seized up. He couldn't

verbalize what he was thinking. He couldn't *think* what he was thinking—that if he were in Bannister's place, he'd make Cat his and never let her go.

"What I would do isn't the issue," Brody said, leaning back against the counter and folding his arms over his chest. "I'm not the one who got her pregnant."

Bannister's face lit up in a huge grin. "Cat's pregnant? That's great!"

Brody straightened. "Wait a minute. She said she *told* you. Are you telling me you didn't know?"

"No, but I'm really happy for her. I know how much she wanted a baby. And Brigit didn't even let on, the little witch. All she said was that Cat was working with you and she gave me this address. Is she here? I'd like to congratulate her."

Brody sagged against the counter, squeezing his throbbing head, struggling to make sense of this conversation. "Listen, why don't you just kick my ass and let me get back to my coma?"

Bannister came to his feet. "You know what? Forget about the coffee. Looks to me like you could use the whole pot, anyway. I take it Cat's not here?"

"Not till noon."

"Too bad. Tell her I came by. I was going to reschedule our date, but I see I'm no longer needed." He gave Brody's shoulder a good-natured whack.

"What date? No longer needed for what?"

"To get Cat pregnant. Looks like she managed

without me. Mistaken identity," he said with a chuckle. "That's a riot."

Why was the guy smiling? "You're telling me…you're not the father?"

"I don't know what she told you, but I only met Cat once, and that was twenty years ago. She and my cousin Brigit called me a couple of months back and arranged our—" he did a lazy hip thrust "—baby-making date. I was kind of looking forward to it—Cat was a cute little thing back then, even with the granny glasses—but the blackout stranded me in Boston."

"A baby-making date? She *wanted* to get pregnant?"

"In the worst way. But I take it she's never found a guy worth settling down with, so she decided to go solo."

Cat had been *trying* to get pregnant that night. She'd lied about being on the Pill. Brody's mouth went dry. His ears buzzed.

Bannister said, "Listen, I was just having a little fun before. You started spilling your guts, and it was good juicy stuff, so I just kind of played along. I would've liked details, but I'll get those from Brigit."

Brody found his voice. "Uh, Greg, do me a favor? Don't tell Brigit you spoke to me." It would get back to Cat, and he needed time to come to grips with what he'd just learned.

"No problem." Laughing, Bannister swatted Brody on the back again, nearly knocking him down. "Mistaken identity! I'd love to stay and hear her side, but I've gotta run."

Brody followed the man who wasn't Cat's

lover to the front door and watched him climb into his rental car. He reentered the house zombielike and shuffled to a stop in the kitchen.

"My baby," he said, and the words—even his voice—sounded alien to his ears. "*My* baby." In the corner, Spot raised his head; his sad amber eyes tracked his master's movements as Brody paced restlessly between the sink and the far wall.

He felt disembodied, strangely numb, as if the truth were too immense to get his brain wrinkles around. "I'm going to be a father."

Brody wrenched open the back door and stalked across the yard. He leaned both palms on the tall ash fence and stood there, head bowed, gulping air, letting the remarkable notion gel into something he could find a mental place for.

An incredulous half laugh erupted from him and he raised his head, pushed off the fence. Spot was waiting for him, gumming his well-worn rubber ball. Brody wrestled the ball out of his mouth, tossed it across the yard and watched the old boy totter after it.

He'd never considered becoming a father, never even let himself fantasize about it. The responsibility was too awesome. Better to leave it to the undamaged, as he thought of those who'd been raised in normal, loving households. Brody couldn't bear the thought of failing a child as he'd been failed.

As determined as he'd been not to reproduce, Cat had apparently been just as determined to become a mother, even going so far as to arrange to get impregnated by a virtual stranger. Yet as badly as she'd wanted a baby, she'd been distressed to find herself pregnant, after having denied the indisputable symptoms for weeks.

I didn't want it to be true.

She'd wanted it to be true, all right, she just hadn't wanted him to be the father. Her "horrendous mistake" had planted his seed, and she'd disowned that appalling fact as long as possible, until Brody himself had forced her to acknowledge it.

He was barely aware of Spot vying for attention, dropping his ball at his master's feet and whining.

Cat must have been just as convinced as he that he'd make a lousy father. He'd actually begun to buy in to all that nonsense yesterday about how "nurturing" he was, until he'd realized she'd only been trying to spare his feelings. *Maybe I just hate to admit some people are a lost cause.*

Yep, that was him. Brody Mikhailov, Lost Cause.

Spot let out a single bark. When Brody looked at him, he perked up, tail wagging.

"At least you love me, right, boy?" he murmured, disgusted by his descent into self-pity. He plucked the slobbery ball out of the grass and threw it toward the house. Spot took off.

Until a short while ago, Brody had envied Bannister. He'd envied him not only Cat's loving devotion but even his impending fatherhood and the indelible bond it created with the mother of his child.

With Bannister out of the picture, Brody should have been able to plug himself in to that blissful scenario. Except that without the loving devotion, the rest kind of fell apart.

Cat didn't want him. She'd done everything in her power to push him away, from concocting a bogus boyfriend to withholding the remarkable fact that Brody was going to be a father.

He should despise her for that, but how could he? She was doing what she felt was best for her child, something he could never fault her for. God knew he'd done nothing to alter her opinion of him. She was offering him an easy out with her lies and evasions, and the sensible course of action was to take it.

So that was it, then. He was going to let her go to raise their child alone. He was going to let his son or daughter grow up never knowing his or her father, as Brody had never known his own dad. Of course, it was possible that Cat might eventually find some "guy worth settling down with," as Bannister had put it, and Brody's child would call some other man Daddy.

"Over my dead body."

Spot seconded this with a lively yip. Brody snatched up the ball, hurled it and watched it sail over the fence into the neighbor's yard. Spot came to a wobbly halt at the fence and sent his master a look of studied exasperation.

"Sorry, boy." Brody headed toward the house with long-legged strides that belied his thumping hangover. "I'll fetch it later. Right now I've got too much to do."

11

"YOU'RE WRITING a *coffee-table book?*" Cat stared dumbstruck at the stacks of notes, clippings and folders occupying every square inch of available space in the computer room.

"Don't call it that!" Brody removed his gold-rimmed reading glasses, drawing Cat's attention to his eyes, puffy and red veined. The bottle of get-the-red-out eyedrops sitting on the computer was clearly unequal to the task. His face appeared washed-out beneath his tan. If not for the fact that she'd found him hard at work when she'd arrived—a first—Cat would have sworn he was suffering a hangover.

Then again, perhaps not. He was clean-shaven, which was remarkable in itself. And he was actually wearing shoes—well, sockless sneakers—which he almost never did at home. His hair was wet and he smelled of shampoo and mouthwash.

"Are you sick?" She felt his forehead. No fever.

"I feel fine." His chipper grin looked forced.

She perused the research materials spread out around her, on a subject Brody had once claimed was purely a casual interest. Jerry Lewis, Robin

Williams, Woody Allen, the Marx Brothers, Imogene Coca...

"Why the about-face?" she asked. "I thought you were dead set against doing a book about the comic greats."

"To tell the truth, it's been sort of percolating in the back of my mind ever since we discussed it. When *Banner Headline* didn't work out, I guess I started reevaluating my career."

"What about *Demonic!*?"

He shrugged. "I can always go back to it."

"Have you talked to Leon about this?"

"What are you trying to do, discourage me? I thought you wanted me to expand my horizons."

"I do, it's just...well, it's just awfully sudden."

"You don't have to look so suspicious. I thought people were allowed to grow, to explore their full potential."

"I'm sorry. I didn't mean to... You're right. Forget I said anything. Need any help?"

Brody put his hand on her shoulder. "How are you feeling?"

She touched her slightly queasy stomach. "Fair to middling. I could use a cup of peppermint tea."

"I'll make it."

"Don't be silly. You're in the middle of—" But he was already on his way down the stairs.

In the kitchen Cat watched Brody put water on to boil and set out the tea things, using the last of the peppermint tea bags. She went to toss the empty cardboard package into the garbage—and froze with her foot on the trash can's pedal, holding the lid open. There, on top of the eggshells and banana peels, was an unopened carton of cigarettes, Brody's brand, along with two sealed packs and a half-full one. She glanced on top of the refrigerator. The pack he always kept there was gone.

He must have quit. Strange—he'd never mentioned wanting to. He'd always been as unapologetic about his smoking habit as he was about his career. Could this have something to do with his sudden desire to "explore his full potential"? What other surprises did he have in store for her?

Cat's gaze homed in on the door to the freezer.

"One teaspoon of honey, right?" Brody asked, his back to her.

"One and a half." She opened the freezer. Ice trays. Three cans of margarita mix. A pile of Milky Ways. She peered into the back. A box of frozen waffles. Spot's veal cutlets and Brody's steaks and pork chops. A forlorn box of freezer-burned peas and carrots.

"What are you looking for?" Brody asked, coming up behind her.

Vodka. "A Milky Way. On second thought, that's probably not what my stomach needs right now." She closed the door as the teakettle whistled. There'd always been a bottle in the freezer. Until today. Where had this frenzy of self-improvement come from?

More to the point, how long was it likely to last?

"You didn't answer me," she said. "Can I help you with your new writing project?"

"I had something else in mind for my office mom today." He handed her the mug of tea, opened a drawer and pulled out dozens of scraps of paper, dumping them on the table: index cards, napkins, receipts, yellowed notebook paper, pages torn from magazines and newspapers.

"What's all this?"

"Recipes. Everything I've accumulated since—well, since forever. I've never organized it. Now that you've got me cooking, it's hell trying to find the one I need."

She riffled through the mound of papers. Black bean chili. Chocolate trifle. Herbed beer bread. Smoked Cajun brisket. Seafood paella. A few were from publications, but most were scribbled by hand. "Where'd you get all these?"

He shrugged. "My poker and fishing buddies. People I've interviewed over the years. Girlfriends. All the Spanish dishes are from Leon and his wife, Mercedes. They're world-class cooks."

"Some of these are practically falling apart, Brody. What exactly do you want me to do with them?"

"Mercedes gave me a computer program to record recipes a couple of years back. Calculates nutritional data and everything. I thought maybe you wouldn't mind typing all these in." He gave her his most beguiling smile. "It's indoor work, no heavy lifting."

Cat lifted a recipe written in purple ink in a

feminine hand on a card imprinted with the words *From Tiffany's kitchen*. Somehow she doubted Tiffany was one of Brody's fishing buddies. The recipe was for something called Death by Chocolate.

"Why not?" she said. "Maybe I can make a copy for myself while I'm at it." She grinned at him, recalling their conversation at the amusement park. "You know, with all these recipes, you *could* write a cookbook!"

He scowled. "I'll stick to coffee-table books for the time being."

CAT STOPPED DEAD at the entrance to Brody's dining room. "What happened here?"

He looked up from the three butterscotch-colored candles he was lighting, set in a modern wrought-iron candleholder situated between two formal place settings facing each other. She recognized the boldly patterned dishes and handwoven place mats—she'd helped him pick them out. The cherry-wood tabletop gleamed. A hint of lemon oil underscored the delectable aromas drifting from the kitchen. It smelled like Chinese takeout, only better.

Brody shook the flame off his match. "I moved all those cartons of books up to the guest room. Thought it might be nice to get my dining table back."

"So that's why I heard you running up and down the stairs." For most of the day they'd worked side by side in the computer room, she at the computer, typing recipes, while he organized his new book. He'd knocked off a couple of hours earlier, and now she knew why.

Cat crossed the dining room, admiring Brody's efforts. "Looks like you've been a very busy boy. Whatever you're cooking, it smells outrageous."

"Cold sesame noodles, chicken with cashews, shrimp fried rice and hot-and-sour soup."

"I've been wondering if you knew how to use that wok. And then I came across all those Chinese recipes today. You've been keeping secrets from me!" She touched the rim of a plate. "You went to so much effort, Brody."

"It's Friday," he said, his expression pensive. "I thought it would be nice to share a special meal."

In the subdued light, his eyes were polished onyx. Cat's first glimpse of those eyes, in the dark apartment the night of the blackout, had unnerved her. It was as if some part of her had known that she'd never laid eyes on this man before that night, that this wasn't Brigit's Cute Cousin from Alaska.

Yet another part of her had pushed the knowledge away, out of reach of her conscious mind. Something in those eyes had drawn her then, as it did now.

One week from today, Cat would look into those fathomless eyes and say goodbye forever. She dropped her gaze to the elegant table he'd set, the shapes now blurred, the candle flames distorted by brimming tears. She took a deep breath, grateful for the low lighting.

Brody pulled out a chair. "I hope you're hungry."

She offered a wobbly smile and sat down. "Starved."

WHEN CAT ARRIVED at Brody's house at noon on Monday, she was surprised to find his housekeeper on her way out. Betty usually came on Tuesday and Friday afternoons.

"He wants me here every morning now." The burly middle-aged woman jerked her thumb at the house. "At eight a.m. I figured no way he'll be conscious at that hour, but I was wrong. He's been up since six, working."

"Brody? I don't believe it."

Betty shambled toward her car. "You won't recognize the place."

Brody answered the door on the first ring. "I hate weekends," he said, and kissed her lightly on the lips. "Two whole days without you—it never gets easier."

She chose not to remind him that after Friday, he'd have a lifetime without her. "You're having Betty come every day now?"

"I want to keep the place up."

Cat followed him from the porch, which was as messy as ever, into the living room. "Oh. Oh my."

All the frilly, traditional furnishings were gone. In their place were the dramatic yet comfortable pieces she'd helped him select: contemporary sofa and chairs in candy-apple red leather; tables and wall units in black lacquer and smoked glass. The walls were still waiting to be painted white and the windows were bare, but with its floors sanded and bleached, and devoid of its previous clutter, the room looked…

"Fabulous," she breathed. "Oh, Brody, it's all coming together."

"You ain't seen nothin' yet."

She followed him into the den, where the old plaid-upholstered furniture had been replaced by sleek, modern pieces in rust and navy. The one working television, as well as the VCR and stereo system, had been moved into the new blond-wood entertainment unit. Brody's exercise equipment, which had been upstairs, now occupied one corner of the den.

"What did you do with the tower of TVs?"

"Threw them away. Along with all those broken-down appliances I've been hoarding. Anything that worked, I gave to Goodwill, along with the old furniture. Got rid of it all Saturday morning—the new stuff was delivered in the afternoon."

"And on Sunday you rested," she joked.

"No, on Sunday I had the organizer here. Greta." He ushered Cat out of the den and toward the stairway, now miraculously free of clutter. "Had to pay her double for a last-minute weekend job, but it was worth it."

"The organizer? Is that like the Equalizer?"

"You're not far off," he said, taking the stairs two at a time. "Greta's like a storm trooper with a measuring tape. She scares me. Leon told me about her. She studies your home, workplace, whatever, and shows you how to rearrange things, store things, what to toss out, stuff like that." He stepped through the doorway of the computer room.

Cat joined him, and gaped in awe. "Holy cow." It was an office. A real office. Of the original furniture, only the huge, battered steel desk remained, except now its top surface was visible. She saw a new black leather desk chair, computer workstation, filing cabinet, shelves and a spacious worktable with cubbies to keep work in progress neat and organized.

Not so much as a paper clip was out of place. A big round wall clock ticked off the minutes.

"Greta and I went shopping," Brody said. "What do you think?"

"Holy cow," Cat repeated. "What did you do with all the…"

"Crap. The word you're groping for is *crap*. Whatever needed to be saved now resides in that." He pointed to the filing cabinet. "Amazing invention. Who knew?"

"How did you get the new things delivered so fast?"

In answer he rubbed his fingertips. The green stuff. "Greta didn't stop here. She turned the guest room into a supply and storage room—installed all kinds of racks and cabinets and what all. And that—" he nodded across the hall to what he'd once described as a combination gym, music room and library "—is now strictly a library. I'm going to move the books that are on the porch up here, those I need access to. The rest will go into long-term storage in the attic. It won't be long before the porch actually looks like one."

"Well, I must say, I'm impressed."

Brody sat on the edge of his desk and beamed with pride. "Bet you never thought you'd see the day."

"Do you think it'll last?" she asked.

He glanced around his newly streamlined work space, clearly giving her question some thought. "Yes." He looked at her, his expression at once candid and resolute. "You've never seen me when my mind's made up about something, Cat."

He was drawing a line in the sand. In that instant she knew that her earlier suspicions had been on target. All these positive changes had something to do with her. She wanted to shake him, knock some sense into him.

Don't do this for me, she wanted to tell him. *In five days I'll be out of your life.*

12

CAT UNROLLED ONE of the warm washcloths the
waiter had brought and scrubbed barbecue
sauce off her fingers. "If Nana knew we were on
kind of a date during work hours, she'd have a
conniption. Remember her warnings about 'excessive familiarity'?"

Brody tucked his credit card back into his wal-
let and pocketed it. "Honey, maybe you weren't
paying attention, but we passed the point of excessive familiarity a couple of months ago. And
this isn't 'kind of a date,' it's a date."

He rose and ushered her through the popular
restaurant, which was packed even on this
Wednesday night, thanks to its peerless smoked
ribs and golden hush puppies with maple butter. They emerged on Forty-fourth Street, a half
block from Broadway, where they'd attended a
matinee performance of *Les Misérables*.

Cat had come into Manhattan by train that
morning. Brody had driven in and met her at
Grand Central Station. They'd taken in the latest
exhibit at the Guggenheim and strolled through
Central Park while lunching on hot dogs and
soft pretzels from vendor carts.

It was now nearly 9:30 p.m. and the sky had
gone fully dark while they'd been inside the res-

taurant. Down the street, the lights of Broadway beckoned. Brody asked, "How about we go somewhere quiet for a drink?" Then he remembered. "A couple of virgin daiquiris? Or maybe some decaf cappuccino?"

"It's been a long day. I've enjoyed it, but I'm pooped."

Brody faced her fully, his hands on her shoulders. "Are you feeling all right? We overdid it, didn't we? Are those ribs sitting okay?"

"I'm fine. Really. Just a little tired. I think I should head home."

"You know, the Marriott's right around the corner." And his neighbor George was taking care of Spot, so Brody could stay out all night. "Hey, don't look at me like that. I'm only trying to spare you the long ride to Tarrytown."

It was almost true. They hadn't made love since that time last Thursday when he'd jumped her in the bathroom. He wanted her so badly it hurt, but he drew the line at pressuring an exhausted pregnant woman for sex.

Cat studied his expression as if gauging his sincerity. Some of it must have come through, because she squeezed his arm and offered an apologetic smile. "Thanks, but I'd rather be in my own bed."

"Let's go then." He put his arm around her and steered her away from Broadway toward the parking spot he'd miraculously found three blocks away.

"Brody, you don't have to drive me. I can take the train."

"Right. I might let you take public transportation all the way to Westchester at night when you're carrying—" *My baby.* He almost said it. "I'm driving you, Cat. This is nonnegotiable."

The fierce protectiveness Brody felt was as novel as it was alarming. Did all expectant fathers feel this way?

He knew she didn't think of him as an expectant father, not in the full sense. What would she say, he wondered, if he told her he'd found out the baby was his? What would she do? More than likely she'd become defensive and shut him out for good. The last thing he wanted was to scare her off.

Brody was hoping to avoid that kind of confrontation. He was hoping she'd come clean on her own, trust him enough to reveal the truth. But they had only two more days together. If it didn't happen within the next two days, he'd have to take drastic action.

This was his baby, damn it, and this was his woman, too, whether she knew it or not! Letting her walk out of his life was not an option.

He knew she thought he was trying to prove something to her with his flurry of self-improvement. She was only half-right. He was trying to prove something to both of them. He still didn't know if he had what it took to be a decent dad, but at this point he knew he had to try. If he let Cat and their child slip away without a fight, he'd never forgive himself.

When they reached his Boxster convertible, Brody lowered the top, taking advantage of the clear and balmy early September night. Cat directed him to take the Henry Hudson Parkway north to the bridge of the same name. "In the Bronx it becomes the Saw Mill River Parkway. I'll tell you when to cut west to Tarrytown."

"That's a heck of a drive every day out to Long Island. How come you always refuse to stay over?" he asked, weaving around midtown traffic as he headed toward the Upper West Side. "It would make it so much easier on you."

"I believe your guest bed has been carted away."

"Only four days ago." He sent her a sardonic look. "And after last Thursday, don't talk to me about separate bedrooms."

"I never stayed because I was afraid we'd do exactly what we did last Thursday."

Brody considered her newfound candor a good omen. He decided to see how far he could push it. "I understand," he said. "You didn't want to be unfaithful to Greg."

She stared straight ahead. Brody waited. His fingers tightened around the steering wheel.

Finally she said, "That's not a problem anymore."

"Why not?"

"We…broke up. Greg and me."

A satisfied smile tugged at Brody's mouth. The fictional boyfriend had obviously been a shield to keep him at a distance. Cat wasn't exactly coming clean, but this was a step in the right direction.

"Mind if I ask why?" he said.

She pushed her windblown hair behind her ears. "I guess we just…didn't hit it off as well as we'd thought we would."

"And the baby?"

Say it, he silently pleaded. *Trust me. I won't let you down.* He wished he could believe that last part. And if he couldn't believe it, how could he expect her to?

Cat kept her gaze glued to the windshield. "Nothing's changed as far as the baby's concerned. I'm going to raise her myself, like I said."

Brody switched lanes abruptly, and had to stop short to avoid a fender bender. His arm shot out in front of Cat. He asked, "You okay?" She nodded.

They lapsed into silence. The car merged with parkway traffic and they sped north along the west side of Manhattan.

At last Brody said, "Her?"

"What?"

"You said you'd raise 'her' yourself."

Cat's voice held a smile. "I keep thinking of the baby as a girl."

A girl. A little girl clambering onto her daddy's lap. Gazing at him with adoring eyes. "What color are her eyes?"

She chuckled self-consciously. "Blue."

"I don't know. If I recall the genetics section of Bio 101, blue eyes are recessive. If one parent has brown eyes, the baby most likely will, too. What color are Greg's eyes?" *Brown.*

"Uh..."

"Don't you know?" They'd met once, Bannister had said, twenty years ago.

"Of course I know. They're blue. Dark blue."

"Oh, that's right. You said I look a lot like him.

Startling resemblance, I think you said. Which was why you mistook me for—"

"I remember," she snapped.

"So your little girl might very well come out looking like me." Brody sensed Cat's sudden tension. "I bet it'll almost look like I'm her dad."

I can't make it any easier for you, he thought. *Say it.* But she remained silent.

"Speaking of kids," he said at last, as he shifted lanes to pass a sluggish Buick. "Maybe it's you being pregnant and all that got me thinking about it. I know I came across as...well, I know how I came across, but that's not totally accurate. Not by a long shot."

"What are you talking about?"

Brody gripped the wheel with sweat-slick fingers. "Kids. I mean, I know what I said, all right? But I've been thinking. I'm not against having them."

"Well, that's a relief for those of us who are having them."

"No, I mean...what I mean is, I'm not against *me* having them. Not that it would be, you know, *me* actually having them, but a, you know..."

"A woman."

"*My* woman. Having them for me. With me." He broke off with a muttered oath. His chest had become a pinball machine. He hadn't had a drink or a smoke in six days, and he sure as hell could've used both right then.

She said, "Wasn't it less than a week ago that you were saying—"

"I changed my mind, okay?"

Brody could almost hear her thinking *lost cause*. He glanced at Cat. She was looking at him now, listening attentively. He forced himself to take a deep breath, forced his hands to relax on the wheel.

"I have a few hang-ups about this stuff," he said, and did a mental double take, realizing he'd summed it up in a nutshell. "I never thought of it that way before. I guess it's easier to point out my office mom's insecurities than to recognize my own." He sent Cat a lopsided smile.

She said, "If I'm insecure about marriage and the whole nuclear-family thing, I have good reason to be."

"I never said you didn't. It's human nature to learn from negative experiences, so you can avoid them in the future. All I'm saying is we don't have to let our caution overwhelm our judgment. And I think both of us have been guilty of that."

"I didn't make my decision lightly, Brody—to raise my child alone."

"I know you didn't, honey. I know you want what's best for your baby. And you'll make a terrific mother no matter what." He steeled himself. "But what if the father of your child *wanted* to be involved? What would you do then?"

Cat was silent as they left upper Manhattan and entered the Bronx, crossing the bridge where the Harlem River meets the Hudson. Finally she said, "It doesn't bear discussion. He's out of the picture."

Was Cat talking about Brody or Greg? The

urge to set her straight was overpowering. The father of her child was most definitely not out of the picture. With every day that passed, Brody's determination ratcheted up another notch.

He asked, "And if he offered to marry you?"

"I think…I think I'd have to say no. He's not the kind of man I'd consider marrying, or raising a family with."

Now Brody knew she was talking about him. Cleaning up his act hadn't made much of an impact, apparently. He wished he knew what else he could do. "Sometimes we have to take what life hands us, Cat. It's not always what we had in mind, but it usually has a way of working out."

"Still trying to throw me at Greg?"

Brody ground his teeth to keep from blurting out something he'd regret. When he didn't answer she said, "So. You've decided you want kids, after all?"

"No. What I've decided is I'm not going to let a couple of pathetic screwups make the decision for me."

"Which pathetic screwups might these be?"

"My worthless drunk of a mother and the careless son of a bitch who planted me in her belly." Cat flinched, but he plowed ahead. "I've decided not to follow your gutless example, Cat. If I choose not to have children, it won't be because those two losers made a mess of it."

Her voice shook. "You have no right to call me gutless. I want a baby—this baby—more than anything. I haven't let my parents' mistakes scare me away from motherhood."

"No, you've let them scare you away from

marriage. Raising children is a matter of team-work. It should be, anyway."

"I have nothing against marriage. I just haven't found the right man."

"How long have you been looking?"

"Twenty years."

"You're telling me that in two decades of diligent man-hunting, you haven't found one guy worth settling down with?" he asked, parroting Greg Bannister's words.

"I have standards. What's wrong with that?"

"You tell me. Are these standards attainable by a mortal male in one lifetime?"

She responded with a disgusted growl. "You sound like Brigit."

"I'm liking this Brigit more and more."

Brody didn't pursue the subject. He'd given Cat something to think about, and that was enough for now.

After a long silence she startled him by asking, "Do you really consider yourself responsible for Serena Milton's suicide?"

"Where did that come from?"

"You don't have to answer if you don't want to."

"I don't mind," he said, and found to his surprise that it was true. Which didn't make it any easier to put his feelings into words. He kept his eyes on the road. "I've asked myself that question a hundred times, Cat. I've examined that whole horrible mess from every conceivable angle." He took a deep breath. "I dream about it." He'd never told that to anyone.

Just when he'd decided she wasn't going to

respond, she said, "You once told me that driving Serena to suicide was your finest career move."

He grimaced at the memory.

She said, "After I got to know you a little better, I figured out what made you say that."

"Care to enlighten me?"

"It was a smoke screen. It was easier letting me think the worst of you than admitting that you're carrying around all this guilt."

"Maybe I was just trying to get a rise out of you." He glanced at her. "As I recall, it worked."

"I bought in to your bluster back then. I didn't know you very well. I wouldn't fall for the same nonsense now."

"I stand forewarned."

"It wasn't your fault, you know."

"Look," he said, "I know you mean well, but—"

"She'd been on the brink for years, Brody. Didn't one of her ex-husbands say she'd tried it before?"

"That was a cry for help. It wasn't a genuine suicide attempt."

"If you say so, Dr. Mikhailov. Though if you ask me, washing down a few dozen pills with a quart of Southern Comfort sounds more like a bungled job than a cry for help. All I know is the woman had been certifiable for as long as anyone could remember. She'd made a wreck of her life and told anyone who would listen that she intended to end it all—*before* your stupid book hit the shelves. So I don't want to hear about your stupid guilt!"

Brody couldn't decide whether to laugh or kiss her. Just when he'd concluded that the mother of his unborn child had absolutely no faith in him, she had to go and throw him this curve ball.

Grinning, he said, "So what you're saying is I don't need to worry that my stupid books might actually influence a reader in any meaningful way. It's not as if they're *real* books."

"Mind candy. Don't give it another thought."

The rest of the drive went quickly as they made their way through the Bronx and Westchester. Cat directed Brody to a well-kept two-family house on a quiet block in Tarrytown.

"My apartment is upstairs," she said.

The upper floor was dark, and Brody thought how lonely Cat must be living here. Of course, he had an entire house to himself, bigger than this one, but he was a solitary type. Cat was a people person; she thrived on human companionship.

"Thanks so much for the ride, Brody. And the whole day. It was...it was very special." She kissed him on the cheek, as if this were their first date.

This *was* their first date, he realized with a start.

When she began to pull away, Brody gently drew her back. He kissed her, a real kiss, tender and deep. He put everything into this kiss that he couldn't put into words, all his heartache and yearning, his awe for the miracle of new life that both bound them and tore them apart.

When at last they separated, Cat was trembling. Brody's raw, unspoken feelings threatened to choke him.

She pulled away and reached for the door handle. Her voice wobbled. "My landlady's probably watching."

He took a deep breath, let it out. "Should've left the top up." She started to open the door and he stopped her. "Let me stay with you tonight."

Her sad gaze caressed him. "You can't. My landlady, Mrs. Santangelo..."

"To hell with Mrs. Santangelo. I want to sleep next to you, Cat." He captured her hand. "I want to wake up next to you." *Tomorrow morning and every morning.* "We don't have to do anything. I know you're tired."

The nearest street lamp was some distance away; shadows shrouded her face, but they couldn't conceal the chaos of emotions assailing her.

"Cat..."

"No, Brody. I'm sorry. I wish...I wish things were different."

She wished *he* were different. She withdrew her hand from his and let herself out of the car.

He walked her to the front door. He touched her cheek, a feather stroke, but didn't kiss her again. They said good-night and she disappeared into the house.

Brody sat in his car and watched until a light went on upstairs. Her shadow passed the closed curtain. He turned the key in the ignition and pulled away from the curb.

13

A BEER STEIN of buttermilk, enough to make a thick batter

Cat squinted at the barely legible pencil scratchings scrawled on the back of a receipt for an oil change, and continued to type the ingredients list for "Harry's Kick-Ass Cornbread."

A handful of dried onion flakes

Whose handful? she wondered. One of this Harry's probably equaled two of hers.

Optional ingredients: chopped jalapeño peppers, corn scraped off the cob, shredded jack or cheddar cheese, cooked bacon bits...

She glanced across the computer room to where Brody sat at his worktable, poring over his notes for the book on comic actors. He was facing her, but his attention was on the papers spread out before him.

As always when he worked, he wore his gold-rimmed reading glasses, a concession to his forty-year-old eyes. Surprisingly, she found the glasses actually enhanced his physical appeal. Perhaps it was the air of scholarliness they imparted, or even the hint of vulnerability, so at odds with his robust masculinity. The contrast had been even more marked before last Friday, when he'd sported perpetual razor stubble. The effect wasn't the same now that he was clean-shaven.

Cat allowed herself a wry grin, amused by the fact that she actually missed that scruffy razor stubble. She leaned back in her chair, watching Brody work. He'd made every effort to tidy himself up, but nothing could make his short, dark hair lie flat on top. She was gratified to see he still had something of the lost boy about him.

This train of thought was both surprising and sobering. Before she'd met Brody, Cat never would have suspected that less-than-meticulous grooming habits could hold any sort of appeal. A shrill inner voice sounded the alert: there she went again, turning faults into virtues, recasting the father of her child into something he wasn't. At the same time, another inner voice, faint yet persistent, urged her to strip away her preconceived notions and heed her gut instinct.

Her list of requirements for a potential mate was exhaustive, but they boiled down to a few crucial qualities: dependability, integrity, steadfastness and solid values. She'd always considered certain life-style indicators a positive sign, among them a well-respected career, ambition, a neat appearance, gentlemanly manners, self-restraint and punctuality.

Unfortunately, this system was fallible. How many fastidious, well-mannered, temperate, punctual, successful professional men had she gone through during the past two decades? They'd all seemed perfect at first, but when she'd scratched the surface, she'd discovered such charming traits as insensitivity, faithlessness, narcissism, stinginess, a high-maintenance ego, and worst, a low regard for women in general and herself in particular. Outward appearances, she'd learned, were deceiving.

But the greatest roadblock to happily-ever-after wasn't the guys she'd been dating, it was her own warped expectations. Cat could no longer deny the obvious: she was impossible to please. In those rare cases when a man actually lived up to her exacting standards, she went to great lengths to find some disqualifying feature. He spent too many hours at work. He had an overbearing mother. His kids from his first marriage were a handful. In one case she'd dumped a boyfriend because he'd overtipped an attractive, flirtatious waitress.

Brody was right. She was afraid of marriage. Why else would she have spent twenty years subverting her relationships?

A few days ago Brody had undergone a metamorphosis. He'd overhauled his career, his home and his personal habits, as if checking them off one by one on her master list. Yet beneath the skin, he was the same man.

As for the fundamental qualities of dependability, integrity, all of that, she'd be lying if she claimed Brody fell short. In his own inimitable way, he exemplified those virtues, plus a few that had never made it to her list but probably should have: emotional supportiveness, generosity, selflessness, loyalty and a sense of humor. And without a doubt, he respected her.

Just last night he'd claimed he wasn't averse to having children. Even as she wondered what prompted such a dramatic change of heart, she didn't doubt he'd be a fierce defender and provider of any child he was responsible for, particularly in view of what he himself had gone through as a kid.

Brody thought the baby she carried belonged to another man. Yet he'd been actively wooing her since last Friday, with that romantic dinner, yesterday's date in the city, even his campaign of self-improvement. Cat found herself at the center of an elaborate courtship ritual, and she was touched. It wasn't as if he needed to wine and dine her to get her into bed! Nevertheless, as it stood now, they'd never see each other again after tomorrow. Neither of them had made any mention of a serious involvement.

And if he broached the subject, how would she respond? So much had changed during the past two months. She found herself questioning personal convictions she'd once considered carved in stone. Was it the pregnancy? Hormonal upheaval? Could she even trust her judgment at this point?

Brody muttered, "What the hell...?" and pawed through the folders in front of him. He was wearing an old T-shirt, frayed around the neckhole, with a tiny rip in one shoulder seam. The white shirt featured a design of chili peppers in faded green and red, along with the name of a Dallas Tex-Mex restaurant. Every movement he made, no matter how slight, caused those audacious shoulders to shift and bunch under the thin, worn fabric.

"Brody?"

"Yeah?" He flipped a folder open, scowling at the contents.

"Make love with me."

It took two or three heartbeats for her words to register, then his head snapped up. If she'd known how adorable he looked when he was surprised, she'd have done it more often.

He sat back in his chair. Slowly he removed the glasses and set them aside, never taking his eyes off her. Cat became hyperaware of her accelerated breathing, her thudding heart, a voluptuous heaviness where she needed him most.

She rose and walked around the new computer desk, until she stood directly in front of the worktable where he was seated. The windows were bare; sunlight flooded the room. She started to unbutton her sleeveless pink oxford-cloth blouse.

Brody's eyes tracked her every movement as she shrugged out of the blouse, folded it neatly and laid it on the worktable. He stared at her breasts, fuller now with her pregnancy, practically bursting out of the demi cups of her white lace bra.

Cat reached behind her with both hands. She unhooked the bra and placed it on top of her blouse. Brody's chest rose and fell a little faster. His gaze was a hot velvet caress, coaxing her nipples into stiff peaks, stroking her intimate flesh until it hummed.

She slipped off her tan fisherman sandals. She unfastened her beige linen slacks, stepped out of them and folded them meticulously, adding them to the pile of clothing. Brody surveyed her brazenly from head to toe. His penetrating gaze lingered on the white lace bikini panties. "Take them off."

"I don't think so."

"I thought you wanted a little afternoon delight."

"Maybe I changed my mind." *Ha ha ha.*

She reached for her clothes. Brody moved with astonishing speed, snatching them up and tossing them in a corner, out of reach. He settled back in his chair and said with quiet authority, "Come here."

Her body buzzed with anticipation, yet she made herself take a step backward. She clasped her hands demurely at her waist. "I wouldn't blame you for thinking I'm too aggressive. I just can't seem to help myself, with you sitting there looking so…" She sighed. "I really should get back to work."

Cat turned and resumed her seat behind the computer. The monitor was placed to the side, affording Brody an unimpeded view of her nude torso. Her fingernails clicked on the keyboard as she continued to transcribe Harry's recipe.

Plain cast-iron fry pans are okay, but segmented cornbread pans are best—more crust.

She didn't look at Brody, even when she heard his deep-throated chuckle and "You little tease."

Grease a couple of pans and shove them in a HOT oven. The batter's got to sizzle when it goes in!

Cat heard Brody rise and slowly come around the worktable. Her heart shimmied up her throat. She typed: *Bak until gikden barown,* back-spaced over it and struggled to concentrate on the keys.

Brody circled behind her chair. His warm, humid breath curled over her. Cat slowed down her typing, yet she still made a host of mistakes.

Big, hot hands settled on her shoulders. She sat straighter, trying not to squirm, and typed: *This cornbread is great with red-hot chili and ice-cold—*

He seized her nipples.

—beeeeeeeeeer

Casually he asked, "So you don't think you've put in a full day's work?"

As if she could answer with his callused fingers fondling her, gently tugging, exciting her tender breasts just enough to melt her brain.

"Maybe you're right," he said. "You'd better just sit right here until I decide you can get up."

Brody leaned over her shoulder, ostensibly to get a better look at the computer screen. "Bacon bits, huh? I've got to try that." One hand slid lower, over her rib cage and waist. He caressed the bare skin above her panties. His fingertip teased her navel and she quivered. Cat gave up on trying to sit still. It was all she could do not to leap out of the chair and drag him to the floor.

He said, "Has your belly button always been so sensitive?"

She managed to answer, "I don't know. You're the first one who's ever paid any real attention to it."

"Listen, Cat, here's what you're going to do." Her hands were still poised over the keyboard.

He lifted them and pulled her to her feet. "You're going to go into my bedroom and wait for me on the bed."

"Wait for you? Where will you be?"

"In here, finishing up my work. I'll join you when I'm ready."

Cat stared at him. "You're very good," she breathed, awed by how smoothly he'd trapped her in her own teasing game. The thought of waiting even one more minute was sensual agony, as he no doubt knew.

"Funny. I've always been told I'm very bad." He placed a palm on her back and gave her a little shove toward the door.

"When will you be in?"

He returned to his seat behind the worktable and put on his reading glasses. His devilish smile said it all. "Patience is a virtue."

PATIENCE WAS VASTLY overrated. Cat lay on Brody's high four-poster bed, on top of the biscuit brown, raw silk bedspread. The glowing red numbers on his new digital alarm clock advanced sluggishly: 3:44...3:45...3:46...

There were no longer any magazines or books on the new-and-improved nightstand, nothing with which to distract herself as she lay there thinking about what he was going to do when he joined her. The mild breeze wafting through the open window teased every square inch of bare skin. The tips of her breasts were achingly erect; Brody's phantom fingers tormented them still. The molten fullness between her legs seemed to take on a life of its own, fed by her rioting imagination.

At 3:59 she heard Brody's muffled voice in conversation. He had to be on the phone. At 4:03 his booming laugh carried through the wall separating them. She heard what sounded like a jovial goodbye as he hung up. Silence.

Come to me now. Please come to me.

Cat heard his chair scrape back. *Yes!* Her fingers clutched handfuls of the soft bedspread as his sneakered footfalls crossed the computer room, proceeded into the hallway and approached the bedroom. Suddenly conscious of her appearance, she fluffed her hair around her face, flung an arm artfully over her head and raised one knee in a pose calculated to be both nonchalant and seductive. She stared at the closed door, shivering with anticipation.

Brody's footfalls never slowed as he passed the door and descended the stairs. "Spot!" he called. "Want to go for a walk, boy?"

Cat bolted up and swung her legs off the bed, calling Spot's master every vile name in the book. She stalked to the door, and hesitated with her hand on the knob. If she stayed there and waited like a good little girl, he'd come to her. Eventually. He'd said he would. But if she charged after him like some sex-starved Amazon, what then?

Downstairs, Spot yipped with excitement. She pictured Brody clipping the leash onto his collar. After a minute she heard the front door open and close.

Cat released the doorknob with one last ripe

curse, torn between outrage and giddy laughter. She resumed her place on the bed, occupied by sweet thoughts of revenge, which inevitably took a carnal turn as the minutes ticked by.

By 4:17 she was so aroused that the sound of Brody reentering the house sent a violent tremor through her. After a couple of minutes she heard the staircase creak under his weight. Her breasts quivered with each ragged breath as his footfalls grew louder and finally paused at the closed bedroom door.

Cat stopped breathing. She watched the knob turn. She didn't bother with the provocative pose but simply lay there like some sacrificial victim—waiting to be impaled by the high priest's imperial scepter, she thought, biting her lip against both a hysterical giggle and her remorseless hunger.

The door swung open and Brody entered. Casually he surveyed her form, as if assessing her level of compliance. Cat resisted the impulse to vent her fury. Judging by his droll expression, he was already well aware of her state of mind.

He kicked off his sneakers. "I wouldn't have pegged you as the submissive type." Lazily he pulled off his T-shirt and tossed it onto the floor. "Opens up whole new possibilities I hadn't considered before." He undid his belt buckle. "If you ever get tired of being an office mom, you could always rent yourself out as a love slave."

His heavy-lidded smile and that one arched eyebrow turned the bantering words into an invitation. Cat had no experience with sexual roleplaying—her short stint as Delilah notwithstanding. But if she'd learned anything during the last interminable forty-five minutes, it was that being at the mercy of your lover's whims could be an incredible turn-on.

She felt a little foolish as she played along with the love-slave fantasy. "I'm yours to do with as you will." But then Brody dropped his jeans and briefs, and she forgot to be self-conscious. His extravagant state of arousal mirrored her own. She swallowed hard, unable to tear her gaze from his flagpole erection.

The mattress dipped under his weight as he sat next to her. He leaned over and nudged one puckered nipple with the tip of his tongue. Cat's breath fled in a rush. Her hips rocked. Brody smiled. He continued to lick her with short, searing strokes, as if savoring the taste of her.

"I like this new obedient you," he murmured, switching his attention to the other nipple. He licked it, circled it, drew it into his scalding mouth and lightly bit it, stinging little nips that sent spears of pleasure straight down through her body. Cat was moaning helplessly by the time he raised his head.

Brody cupped his palm over the dark triangle visible through the white lace of her panties. His fingertips fondled the saturated fabric. "You must've been thinking of some very naughty things while you were waiting for me."

"Does that displease you?" she asked meekly.

His roguish smile told her he was enjoying this fantasy play as much as she was. "On the contrary, I expect it. As my love slave, you're required to remain in a state of readiness at all times."

Brody moved to the foot of the bed. Kneeling, he grabbed her thighs and abruptly yanked her down so her feet dangled off the high mattress on either side of him. He bent his head. Cat gasped when she felt his hot breath through the lace—and cried out as his mouth closed over her. Her hips jerked up and she lost the battle to salvage her pride.

"Brody...oh, please, now. *Now!*"

He pinched her bottom, just sharply enough to make her gasp. "Such impertinence will not be tolerated. Your only purpose is to serve my pleasure."

Sure thing, my lord and master. Just you wait until it's my turn to call the shots.

He took his time, nibbling and kissing her through the lace, humming hotly as her body bowed under his mouth. Finally, when she felt ready to explode, Brody hooked his fingers in the bikini panties and pulled them off her.

If she weren't playing the passive love slave, Cat would have locked her legs around him and impaled herself on his imperial scepter without delay. As it was, all she could do was lie there trembling with unappeased need as his fingers parted her and his mouth claimed her once again.

She bucked and twisted under the erotic assault. Her hoarse cries rang in her ears. His lithe tongue licked and flicked and speared her. His mobile mouth captured the ultrasensitive bud with dizzying suction that propelled her hips off the bed.

His hands slid under her bottom, raising her farther as he reared up and drove into her, slowly, a steady, relentless invasion that opened her, stretched her to the point of pain. It was a delicious, welcome pain. He was huge and he was hard and he was just where she needed him to be.

Brody's midnight eyes caught and held her, glittering with a feral light, as if the veneer of civilization had been stripped away to lay bare the primitive male animal within. His face was dark; veins stood out in his neck.

He tilted her hips and thrust home the final distance. Cat screamed as her orgasm struck, a blinding maelstrom of pure, pounding sensation that left her limp and breathless, cocooned in the haven of Brody's strong arms. He pressed kisses to her face, coaxing her back to awareness.

Their legs still hung off the mattress; together they wriggled higher on the bed. Brody smiled at her, a tender smile that she returned as they began to move and found their rhythm. No words were needed to affirm the simple rightness of the moment. It was as if they'd known each other always, been lovers always. It had been that way the first time, and it was that way now.

As their movements grew more frenzied, Brody doubled a pillow and shoved it under Cat's bottom, bracing himself over her. She clung to his arms, corded with hard muscle, and wrapped her legs around his pistoning hips. She met his deep, powerful thrusts as her pleasure spiraled and peaked. Brody was pacing her, she knew, waiting for her.

"Now..." she breathed, as her climax crested. "Now, oh, now..."

He let himself go then, lunging for his own release, shuddering with it even as she toppled over the edge once more.

They collapsed together. Brody immediately lifted his weight off her and rolled to the side.

"It's all right," she mumbled, loving the feel of him pressing her into the mattress.

He placed his palm on her belly. "We have to be careful."

She couldn't suppress a wry grin as she tugged the pillow out from under her. "*Now* you want to be careful?"

He leaned up on his elbow. "Did I hurt you?"

"No! Of course not."

He appeared unconvinced. "Did Dr. Jackson mention any, you know, restrictions?"

"Yes. She said no swinging from the chandeliers."

"She did not."

"Cross my heart. What she meant was nothing too rough." Cat pressed her finger to his lips. "And before you ask, no, you weren't too rough."

Brody swept his gaze over her as if looking for damage. She grabbed the pillow and hurled it into his face.

"Hey!" he bellowed.

"You can't retaliate, I'm pregnant."

"I'll save it all up for when you're not."

In the next instant his smile faded. She made herself say what they both were thinking. "I'll be long gone by then."

His expression was heartbreakingly bleak. "You don't have to be. You know that. You know how I feel about you."

"Brody..."

"Cat, I love you." His voice was hoarse with emotion. "I've never said that to anyone else. I've never felt this way about anyone else. I knew I loved you even before—" He stopped abruptly, and she saw his throat working. Quietly he said, "I've known it for a long time."

Cat reached up and pushed her fingers through his hair, spiky with sweat. She struggled to contain the tears that threatened. "There's the baby," she whispered.

She sensed he was waiting for her to say more. When she didn't, he said, "I'll love the baby, too. I already do." He seized her hand in a grip that was almost painful. "Trust me, Cat."

His expression was so raw, so unguarded, she had to look away. *Trust me.* Would he still love her if he knew how she'd deceived him? She settled for the simple truth, the safe one.

"I don't know what to think anymore, Brody. I'm confused."

He kissed her fingers. "Stay with me tonight."

She looked at him. That was the one thing she'd always refused him, though he'd asked repeatedly. Tomorrow would be their last day together.

He pressed another, lingering kiss to her fingers, never taking his eyes from hers. "Don't think about it," he said. "Just say yes."

"Yes."

14

CAT HEARD THE SCREEN DOOR open and close behind her as she watched Spot hector a squirrel from the base of a hickory tree. The grass under her bare feet was cool and damp with dew. The chilly early autumn breeze raised gooseflesh on her lower legs, the only part of her not swaddled by Brody's thick white terry robe.

She didn't hear him come up behind her, but she sensed his presence. His long arm snaked around her middle, pulling her against the heat of his bare chest. He drew her hair aside and pressed a lingering kiss to the tender spot where her throat met her shoulder. Cat smiled. Her eyes drifted shut and she caressed the arm banding her waist.

Brody's voice was a sleep-raspy mumble. "When did you get up?"

"About an hour ago."

"Couldn't sleep?"

"I just…didn't want to waste any of this day."

His other arm came around her. "You should've woken me."

"You looked so sweet sound asleep. I've never seen you sleep before."

"'Sweet'?" He groaned. "Don't let anyone

hear you say that. I've got a reputation to up-hold."

"Sorry to break the news, but you're not that bad, Brody Mikhailov."

He nuzzled her hair. "Well, maybe a little bad."

"A little bad," she agreed, grinning. "Just enough."

He sighed. "I've got that meeting this morning."

"Charlie Chaplin's cousin?"

"Yep. He's staying with friends in East Hampton. They're expecting me around ten."

She looked at him over her shoulder. "You can't postpone it?"

"He's returning to London tonight. I'll try to make it quick. Should be back by one—two at the latest. I thought I'd make reservations at that new restaurant in Island Park."

She hugged his arms. "Do you mind if we stay home? I'd rather...I don't know, I'd rather throw something together here than go out."

After a moment he said, "So would I. We need to talk."

Cat didn't have to ask about what. They both knew. Their future.

She had to tell him about the baby. She'd come to that decision at daybreak after a long, sleepless night. She only hoped her courage wouldn't fail her. The thought of how Brody would react when he learned of her deception made her weak in the knees. Cat wouldn't blame him if he ended up despising her. She prayed his innate compassion would help him understand her actions and forgive her.

Because the truth was she needed Brody. She needed him by her side, loving her, sharing their child, making a home and a life with her. Nothing had ever felt so right.

"Yes," she said. "We need to talk. There are things…there are things we have to clear up. Before we go any further."

Brody's arms tightened around her, and only then did she realize she was trembling. He turned her face and kissed her lips, a cherishing kiss full of promise. The fan of crinkles at the corners of his eyes deepened with his gentle smile. His eyes were shiny. A trick of the early morning light, no doubt.

"Tonight," she said. "We'll talk tonight. Go on." She made a halfhearted effort to push him away. "You've got to get moving or you'll be late for that meeting."

His hand strayed higher. He squeezed her breast through the thick terry cloth. "Join me in the shower. It'll go quicker if you wash my back."

"Ha ha ha."

His long, callused fingers slipped inside the robe. Her breath snagged. Brody's voice was a sultry murmur. "I'll return the favor, of course."

"You'll wash my back?"

"Let's just say I'll get around to it eventually."

"HEY, KIDDO, how's it shakin'?"

Cat stepped aside and let the man into Brody's house, though she'd never laid eyes on him before. That steel-wool voice kind of narrowed it down. "It's shakin' just fine, Leon."

"Glad to hear it." He handed her a paper sack containing what appeared to be a gift-wrapped liquor bottle, and bent to roughhouse with Spot, sending the old mutt into a delirium of drooling, tail-wagging rapture. Leon didn't look anything like she'd imagined, with his neatly trimmed, snow-white hair and mustache, and impeccable dark suit and tie. He looked at Cat. "That boy been treating you okay?"

She allowed herself a private smile and pushed her hair behind her ears. "Can't complain."

"Not getting fresh, is he? All you gotta do is squeal to that Littlestone broad. She'll have his, uh, she'll have him for breakfast. That lady doesn't fool around."

"Actually, I've been chasing *him* around the desk. Can't seem to keep my hands off him."

Leon roared with laughter. "Yeah, right. Sounds like you can take care of yourself."

"Brody's a lot like Spot here. His bark is worse than his bite."

"I guess so, since you decided to re-up for a second month."

Cat wouldn't call it re-upping. It was more like being drafted. But she didn't correct Leon. The fact was she thanked God Brody hadn't allowed her to desert after that first month of boot camp.

Leon laid his hand on her shoulder. "I want you to know I think you've been just what that boy needed, Cat. I can hear it in his voice. He sounds relaxed. No, not relaxed. Content, that's it. Like something was missing and all of a sudden it just clicked into place."

A sense of purpose, she thought, and wondered if Brody's agent knew about his new book project.

She said, "Come on in, Leon. Can I get you something cold to drink?"

"I can't stay. I guess he's out. Didn't see that fancy-ass convertible of his."

"He's at a meeting—interviewing a source."

Leon's crooked smile spoke volumes. "Tough job, letting lonely baseball groupies cry on your shoulder."

So. Brody hadn't told Leon about the new direction he was taking his career. Perhaps he was waiting until he had a first draft, something solid to deflect the inevitable resistance his agent was sure to throw at him.

Spot was whining for attention. Cat reached down and started rubbing him. "Well, I'll tell him you stopped by."

"I had a reason for stopping by. Wish I could've told him in person." Leon's face split in a huge grin. "You know that TV job? *Banner Headline?*"

Cat's heart stuttered. "What about it?"

"It's his!" Leon crowed. "Mildred Maxwell got herself canned. Brody was right. The silly old broad's a has-been—her last big scoop was about Jackie's inaugural gown. She hasn't got the connections, stomach or stamina to dish serious, network-caliber dirt week after week."

Cat was numb. Spot prodded her limp hand with his nose. "Brody...Brody got the TV job."

"He sure as hell did!" Leon nodded toward the sack she held. "Figured he'd want to celebrate. Just don't let him get ossified. He's gotta fly out to the Coast pronto, and I want him in fighting trim when he gets there."

Leon shook his head in wonder. "I'm telling ya, kiddo, this must be what they call divine intervention. I've known that boy going on twenty years, and I've never seen him want anything the way he wanted this *Banner Headline* gig. Had his heart set on it from day one." Leon peered closely at Cat. "Hey, you okay?"

"Yes. Thanks for coming by, Leon." She held the door open.

"You'll give him the news?"

"I think...I think he should hear it from you."

"Then tell him to page me—he's got my beeper number. Sure wish he'd been home, though. What I wouldn't give to see his face!"

BRODY STOPPED POUNDING on the door to Apartment 4F when a female voice behind it warned him to knock it the hell off or she'd Mace him. He addressed the peephole she was no doubt glaring through.

"I'm looking for Cat Seabright. My name is Brody Mikhailov."

Locks turned and the door creaked open, revealing a frowsy brunette wearing black crushed-velvet pants and a gauzy, eggplant-colored tunic adorned with a quartz crystal necklace. A cloud of jasmine incense hovered around her.

She scrutinized him unapologetically. *"You're* Brody?"

"You must be Brigit." He extended his hand, and she shook it. He asked, "Is she here?"

"Nope."

Brody had arrived home after his meeting to find a note from Cat tucked under a gift-wrapped bottle of vodka, instructing him to call Leon right away. "I wish I could stay and tell you goodbye in person," the note continued, "but I'm not strong enough. It's better this way."

After he'd spoken to Leon, he'd tried calling Cat at her place, but there was no answer. He'd driven to Tarrytown anyway, thinking she might not be answering the phone. Her landlady told him she'd come home briefly and left with an overnight bag. He'd figured it was a good bet she was hiding out with her best friend, so he'd headed to Brigit's apartment in Greenwich Village.

"You don't mind if I have a peek," Brody said, shoving past Brigit into her funky living room. One wall was bare brick; the other three were covered with an ultrarealistic landscape mural, a meadow scene complete with trees, a brook and swaying grasses stretching to the blue horizon. A half-dozen multicolored kites dangled from the high ceiling, which had been painted to resemble a sky full of scudding clouds.

It took Brody a few moments to notice Brigit's

cousin Greg Bannister lounging on a futon, chowing down on a plateful of sushi.

Greg drawled, "Hey, Brody. Pull up some chopsticks. You like yellowfin?"

Brigit gaped at them. "You two know each other?"

Brody ignored them both and stalked down the hall to the solitary bedroom. Deserted. Ditto for the bathroom and tiny kitchen. "Where is she?"

Brigit said, "I told you, she's not here."

"But you know where she is."

"I can't tell you." She looked like she wanted to, though. "She made me promise."

"Listen, I don't know what Cat told you, but I have to talk to her."

Brigit's pout was accompanied by a whine of frustration. "She made me *promise*, Brody. I *can't.*"

"Yes you can! Goddammit, that woman is carrying my baby!"

Brigit gasped. "She *told* you?"

"No." Greg tapped his chest with his shiny black chopsticks. "That would be me."

Brody crossed his arms and stared her down. "The bottom line is I'm not leaving here until you tell me where she is."

"I really want to." Brigit wrung her hands. "But she made me promise."

"She didn't make *me* promise," Greg said, around a mouthful of raw tuna and sticky rice.

Brody whirled on him. "Where is she?"

Greg shrugged. "Beats me."

Brody shoved his fingers through his hair, snarling an oath that made Brigit flinch.

"Are you guys slow learners or what? Brigit didn't promise not to tell *me* where she is," Greg said, indicated himself with an exaggerated gesture, "and I didn't promise not to tell *you*."

"Oh! Yeah, yeah!" Brigit cried, flapping her hands in excitement. "So if I tell you, you can tell—"

"*Just do it!*" Brody hollered.

He watched as Cat's friend went through the asinine ritual of whispering in her cousin's ear. Greg finished chewing and looked up at Brody. "Her agency's apartment. Ye olde love nest."

"Ohh, she's gonna kill me," Brigit whimpered.

15

BRODY STOOD WATCHING Cat sleep, curled on her side on the bed where it had all started two months ago—the bed where they'd conceived their child. He switched on the bedside lamp, banishing the gloom of early evening, and saw that her lashes were damp and spiky; the dried track of a tear marred her cheek.

He remembered making his way into this bedroom back in July, during the blackout, after having been lent the apartment by Nana. His steps had slowed as he'd detected a subtle woodsy-floral fragrance. The meager moonlight had teased him with the merest suggestion of a pale, delicate face, the luminous swell of nearly bare breasts rising and falling in the unhurried cadence of sleep.

It was then that Brody had recalled Amory saying there'd be a "special surprise" waiting for him in the bedroom. Naturally he'd concluded that this luscious lady-in-waiting was a hired pro. He'd sat on the bed and awakened her gently, fully intending to decline her services and bunk on the living room sofa.

Brody smiled, recalling how determinedly—and cleverly—Cat had seduced him. She must have wanted this baby very badly.

He sat next to her now. A strand of wavy red hair had fallen over her lips. He lifted it and stroked it back into place. She stirred slightly.

He leaned over and whispered in her ear. "I love you, Goldilocks."

Her eyelids fluttered—and snapped open when she realized she wasn't alone. As she stared up at him, he watched her initial, drowsy pleasure at seeing him succumb to sorrow.

"I love you," he said. "Don't run from me, Cat. Don't run from *us*."

"Brody. You shouldn't have come here. It makes it so much harder…" Her chin wobbled.

"Did you think I could give you up so easily?"

Cat sat up. She hugged her knees. "I knew Brigit would crack. How did you get in here?"

"Got Amory to give me the keys. They're still looking for the other set." Quietly he asked, "Why did you leave?"

She drew a deep, shaky breath. "I wanted so badly to believe we could make it work. For a while there, I convinced myself it was possible. Then Leon showed up with the news about that TV job, and I realized…I realized I'd lost sight of what you need to make you happy."

"I know what I need to make me happy. I'm looking at her."

"I'm talking about your goals, Brody. You know what you want out of life, out of your career. This TV job will put you on the map. You may not believe this, but I'm happy for you. I know how much it means to you."

"Cat—"

She held up her hand. "You'll be moving to

L.A." Her grimace left little doubt how she felt about the City of Angels. "Writing this show will be like trying to distill one of your biographies into an hour of concentrated mudslinging. Week after week. You'll be under a lot of pressure. If I went with you, I'd be miserable, and you'd resent me more and more."

"And then we'd split up and the baby would suffer."

Her hand went to her abdomen, a reflexive gesture of protection. He'd never loved her more—or felt more exasperated.

He said, "You've got this all worked out, haven't you? The forced move to La-La Land, the sleazy TV job, the fights, the divorce lawyers, the custody battle."

"I'm a realist."

"What if I turned down the job?"

"I wouldn't let you do that. I refuse to stand in the way of your goals."

"You're already standing in the way of my goals if you'd deny me the one thing I need most, which is you."

"You may feel that way now, Brody, but you won't when you're working on your tenth coffee-table book and wondering how your life would have been different if only you hadn't succumbed to temporary insanity."

He spread his arms wide. "Well, call out the fellas in the white coats, then, 'cause I turned down the job."

"What!"

"I told Leon to tell Schneider and that crowd thanks but no thanks."

"You did not!"

"Leon didn't take the news too well, but he'll get over it."

"What *possessed* you to do such a thing?" Cat jumped up off the bed. She snatched the phone off the nightstand and shoved it in his face. "Call him back! Now!"

He leaned against the headboard. "I don't think so."

"Brody!" She shook the phone at him. "Do it! Before he calls those people!"

"You haven't been listening." In a lightning-quick move he grabbed her and flung her into his lap. He wrested the phone from her and tossed it onto the bed. She tried to wriggle out of his grasp, without success. "I don't want the damn job," he said, patiently enunciating each syllable. "I did want it at one time, yes, before I got my priorities straight. Will you just sit still and listen for a second?"

Cat stopped squirming. She sighed in defeat.

"Are you listening?"

"Yes, I'm listening."

"Let's say I take that job on *Banner Headline*," he said, "the one that's too good to turn down. Sooner or later the show gets canceled or they bring in someone hungrier or more ruthless or better connected. And I move on to the next fantastic opportunity that's too good to turn down, and the next and the next. And then one day I look around me and I wonder how my life would be different if only I hadn't succumbed to temporary insanity." He pulled her close and kissed the top of her head. "If only I hadn't given up the only woman I ever loved. And my child."

He was holding her so tight, he felt more than heard her gasp. She looked at him, and in her brimming eyes he read shock. Trepidation. Hope.

"You know," she whispered.

He nodded.

"How...?"

"Greg Bannister came by looking for you. We had us a nice little chat."

Her eyes grew round. "When?"

"Last Friday."

She pondered this. "Right before your remarkable transformation."

"I didn't know how else to prove myself. I know what you think of me, Cat."

"No. You're wrong."

"Come on, honey. You haven't exactly made a secret of it. My career, my life-style. You don't respect anything about me."

"That's in the past. I was an idiot. I was only looking at the superficial stuff. If I'd let myself see beneath the surface..." She shook her head. "You were right. I let my hang-ups make my decisions for me."

"It wasn't just you I needed to prove myself to. I wasn't sure...I'm still not sure I can be a good dad. It'll take a lot more than pouring the booze down the drain and tidying up the house. And I can't promise I've written my last trashy exposé. A guy's got to get dirt under his fingernails once in a while."

"None of that matters." Cat shifted in his embrace to face him. "Brody, don't you see it? Don't you feel it?" She placed her soft hand on his cheek. "You'll make a wonderful father. You have this solid core of…of goodness, of caring. You're the most decent man I know."

He laughed, even as his heart swelled, filling him with warmth. "Me? Decent? Have you read my last few literary masterpieces?"

In response she grabbed his face with both hands and kissed him on the lips.

He said, "You must've missed *Getting Their Kicks: The Secret Lives of the Rockettes.*"

She kissed him again, harder. When he started to respond in earnest, she pulled back and said, "I can't believe you don't hate me. I'd decided this morning to tell you myself—that the baby is yours—but I was so scared. I was praying you'd be able to forgive me."

"Honey, by the time I found out I was going to be a daddy, I was already so out-of-my-gourd in love with you, forgiveness wasn't even an issue. Besides…" He kissed her forehead. "I know why you did it, remember? How could I blame you for wanting to do right by your child? Oh now, honey, don't cry."

Smiling, she plucked at his T-shirt to wipe her eyes. "I just can't believe that after all these years, I finally found the man I've been looking for. I finally found my—"

"Oh, please don't say it."

"—Mr. Perfect."

He groaned. "That's it. I was going to give you the biggest damn diamond I could find, but now you'll have to settle for this." He dug in his jeans pocket and produced the brass ring he'd gotten at the merry-go-round.

Chuckling, sniffling, Cat twirled it on her finger. "We might have to get it sized."

"Now, this is going to be one hurry-up wedding. I mean like next week. No fussing over flowers and caterers till you're as big as a blimp. I don't want to have to roll you down the aisle."

She clutched her heart. "That's just the most romantic proposal a girl could ask for."

Brody felt his face heat. "Yeah, well, I just wanted everything settled and out in the open."

"In that case, there's one more thing I need to tell you."

"What now?"

Cat curled her arms around his neck. "I love you, Brody Mikhailov. I even love Jake Beckett and the King of Sling. I love you so much it takes my breath away. I still don't know how it happened. Falling in love with my baby's father was *not* part of the plan."

"Honey, if there's one thing I learned during that blackout—" Brody reached for the lamp switch "—it's that anything can happen in the dark."

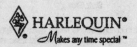

If you enjoyed what you just read,
then we've got an offer you can't resist!

Take 2 bestselling love stories FREE!

Plus get a FREE surprise gift!

COMING NEXT MONTH